With Eyes Open
Gay Romance

Trina Solet

With Eyes Open
Gay Romance

Trina Solet

CHAPTER 1

*I*an watched his father sleeping restlessly in the armchair by the window. He had that ugly, checkered blanket over him, and his eyes and his hands twitched every few seconds. The sunlight coming through the window was weak. Ian worried that his dad might be cold even with the blanket. He got so little sleep these days. Ian didn't want to disturb his rest just to cover him better.

Knowing that his father wouldn't like it if he woke up and found Ian watching over him, he went for a walk.

Soon after coming home from college for the summer, Ian got the bad news about his dad. His dad didn't want to tell him right away. In a small town like Blystone, he had no chance of keeping it a secret. Word got around and eventually Mrs. Lincer stopped Ian on the street. She asked him how his dad was doing and offered to make a "spice tea" for him. She said it was her own special home remedy to help with the nausea from chemo his dad would be starting soon. Ian was stunned, but he managed to thank her anyway. He walked a few steps, then he ran straight home. He got there so out of breath he couldn't even speak to ask his dad why he didn't tell him.

That was at the start of his summer break. Now it was fall,

time for Ian to go back to school, but he was still here. With his dad fighting for his life, Ian wasn't going anywhere.

With his dad resting, Ian decided to go into town. These days he found himself exploring Blystone like he did when he was a kid and this small town was his world. It had seemed immense to him then. Now he could walk from one end of town to the other in ten minutes. The longest part of his walk was getting to the town itself. Ian's house was outside of town, where a handful of big old farmhouses were scattered between fields.

Ian walked along the side of the curving road, glancing at familiar sights as if to make sure they were still there. The ground under his feet was grassy and soft. Shrubs grew further on, marking off the fields. This area was prone to flooding so a ditch ran alongside the road to collect the runoff.

After he passed the bus stop at the crossroads with Stoneway Road, he saw the scarecrowish sight of the makeshift memorial to Lorna Hayes. From there, it wasn't long until he reached the sign that said Welcome to Blystone. That sign hadn't changed for as long as Ian could remember. Once the sign was behind him, he came across the first houses right on the edge of town. These houses were some of the nicer ones in town, with big gardens behind high fences.

One house in particular drew his attention, number 211. Ian had been drawn to that house since he was a kid. The house was old and had stood abandoned for a couple of decades. Some said it was haunted. Of course a kid would be drawn to it. But for Ian, it was more than that. The place called to him and repelled him at the same time.

Recently, the house and the garden had been spruced up for the new owners. The place had a new coat of paint, but the vibe was the same. It pushed and pulled at him. He went closer to where some tall evergreen bushes grew right against the fence.

As he stood out of sight, Ian got his first look at the people who had moved in. Behind a spiked iron fence, a little boy was crawling on the ground while his father sat at the nearby table using a tablet. Ian didn't mean to spy, but seeing a father and son together like that, he couldn't take his eyes off them.

His own childhood came back to him in flashes. He was running through the field behind their house while his father sat on the back porch. He was either reading or writing, and whenever he raised his head, he waved at Ian. This was a very similar scene.

The little boy was blond and about four or five. His father had light brown hair but the same light blue eyes. The man was in his late twenties, dressed conservatively in a white shirt and gray slacks. Not Ian's type, but he was very good looking – slim, broad shouldered, with a sharp jaw and a kissable mouth. He would be OK if he didn't look like a total stiff.

Ian might claim the guy was miles from what he looked for in a guy, but he couldn't quite take his eyes off him until the little boy drew his attention. The boy was bending his head low and peering closely at something. After a little while, Ian realized that the little boy was watching a green bug, one of a few he was likely to find this time of year. Dry leaves from two big trees covered the garden. The little boy lifted them up whenever the bug crawled away to hide under them. Finally losing sight of it, he scrambled around for a while.

"I lost it!" he said and turned to his father like he wanted him to organize a search party.

His father smiled. "You hunt him down. I'm going to go get lunch ready," he said and went inside.

Ian was ready to move on when he saw the little boy turn and gasp. He jumped up and ran to the other side of the garden. There was a stone bench at the end of the garden. It sat under a whitewashed wall that separated the garden from the property next door.

The boy stopped next to the bench and looked up. Ian wondered if there was something on the wall or on the other side that got his attention. There was nothing there, plus the boy seemed to be looking at a spot in midair about five feet off the ground. Then he nodded and said something. He was too far away for Ian to hear the words, but he kept talking. Sometimes he seemed to be listening. Maybe he had an imaginary friend.

Suddenly the boy's father called out from inside the house.

"Toby! Lunch is ready!"

"I have to go," the little boy told his invisible friend loud enough for Ian to hear. As the boy moved to go, he stopped with his arm outstretched backwards. It was almost like someone was trying to hold him back. The boy turned toward the bench again.

"No, I have to go eat lunch now," he said in a plaintive voice. "You don't want me to get in trouble, do you? I'll come back later. I promise."

He still held his hand out then tugged at it like he was wrenching himself free of someone's grip. He pulled his hand back then waved. As the boy ran inside, Ian looked from him to the end of the garden. There was nothing there, of course. He still kept staring even after the boy was long gone. He couldn't quite believe his eyes.

How could a little boy act out a fake struggle so convincingly? Ian would swear that something held on to the little boy's hand, and he had to pull free of it. As he walked away, Ian shook his head. He didn't know what he had just seen, but he decided to go into town and ask a few questions.

*

Toby ran in through the back door like someone was chasing him. Then he tried to take a seat at the kitchen table right away.

"Did you wash your hands?" Jacob asked him though the answer was obvious.

Standing next to his chair, Toby turned his hands over a few times to examine them. "They look pretty clean," he decided.

"They wouldn't under a microscope. You were playing with bugs. Go wash your hands."

Toby huffed like Jacob was being completely unreasonable. When he came back he climbed into his chair. He was about to pick up his sandwich when he looked up from his plate. He eyed his dad suspiciously. He then lifted the top piece of bread and found nothing suspicious. He lifted the lettuce and found it. A tiny slice of tomato was hiding in the middle of his sandwich.

"You're sneaky," Toby said to the tomato and to his dad.

"Give tomatoes a chance. You'll learn to like them," Jacob told him.

"They're wet," Toby complained.

"So is grape juice and you like grape juice," Jacob pointed out.

Toby didn't have an argument to beat that, but he still shook his head. After looking at his juice glass like it had betrayed him, he bit into his sandwich and made a face. In the end, he ate it without too much fuss, tiny tomato slice and all.

Jacob grinned at him, proud of his boy. It wasn't just tomatoes that couldn't keep him down. Toby had adjusted really well to moving to Blystone. It was a big change. Both of them had left behind their friends as well as family. Jacob did have his sister in Lambton, and Toby was making friends fast.

Jacob never expected to be making a move to a small town, but now that he was here, he felt at home. Finding anyone to date was going to be a major challenge. He groaned as he thought of meeting someone online then driving for miles only to meet him in person and feel no connection. But what other choice did he have? In a small town like this, he wasn't likely to turn a corner and run into a man who could capture his heart after so many failed.

CHAPTER 2

As he went in search of information, Ian remembered hearing of one person who had seen something strange at 211. A few months ago, the local handyman, Mr. Vinik, claimed he saw something. He had been hired by the real-estate agent to fix up the place a little, clear the overgrown garden and do some handiwork around the place. Then she fired him when he started talking about the place being haunted.

After asking around for Mr. Vinik, Ian spotted his truck in front of a house on the other side of town. The man himself was up on a ladder. He was a familiar sight – portly, balding, with that puffy, red vest he always wore. It looked like he was cleaning out old Mrs. McKay's gutters.

Ian waited for him to finish then invited him down to Carlton's Bar for a beer. Once they were sitting down with a beer for Mr. Vinik and a coffee for Ian, who was a year shy of drinking age, they talked about his dad's health for a while. Then Ian asked him about what he had seen.

"And why do you want to know about that?" Mr. Vinik asked.

While he was waiting outside Mrs. McKay's, Ian had come up with a reason he hoped was plausible. "It's for school. I wanted to write something for my short story class. I decided on a ghost story, so I wanted to find out about ghosts from someone who has seen them. You did see something, right?"

Mr. Vinik shook his head, and Ian thought he was about to deny it. But he took a swallow of his beer and said, "I saw it, heard it, and felt it down to my bones. It was like cold fingers reached right through me, grabbed onto my bones and shook me up." Mr. Vinik shook his fist in midair to demonstrate.

"And what did you see and hear?" Ian asked.

"The girl, Lorna. That poor thing." Mr. Vinik made a pained face. "She's cold as the grave now, and if you go near her, you'll sure as hell feel it. I didn't see much of her, just enough to know what I was looking at. And I didn't hear her voice exactly. It was more like I stepped into a wind tunnel or something. It was loud. I couldn't breathe. I thought that might be the end of me. But once I got myself inside the house, I was all right again."

"So this didn't happen inside the house?" Ian asked.

"Oh, no. She got to me when I was clearing out the garden in the back. Didn't even get to finish. Ms. Hughes at the real estate office said I must have been drinking on the job and fired me. I was not. I saw what I saw. And if you don't feel like taking my word for it, it's not only me," Mr. Vinik said, getting mad now.

"Who else saw her?" Ian asked.

"Lorna's own grandmother. She didn't outlive her by much, but she saw the girl too. And just like me, nobody believed her either. Everyone figured it was grief talking or that she was losing it."

"So she's been haunting the house since she died?" Ian said, not sure if he could believe something like that. "Tell me more about Lorna, how she ended up dead."

"You've lived here practically all your life. You heard the stories," Mr. Vinik told him.

Ian had, but he wanted his memory refreshed. "I've heard bits and pieces since I was a kid. Put it all together for me."

"Alrighty. Lorna came to live here when she was a little kid, four or five, after her parents died. Her grandmother took her in and raised her. Then Lorna went off to college and came back from college pregnant. Just about the time she was close to deliver, maybe some weeks away, she got killed right outside of town. That was at this time of year twenty years ago now. She did manage to give birth to her baby before she died. You know the spot, where someone put up that memorial." Mr. Vinik pointed through the bar windows toward the west side of town.

"Someone?" Ian said.

"No one knows who. The night before it wasn't there. There were only some flowers that people left right on the ground and a spindly, little, white cross. Next morning, that contraption was up with Lorna's name on it. That's just another unsolved mystery for you. The case of who killed her was never solved either. No wonder she haunts her grandmother's place. Spirits that don't get justice can't rest easy."

"Who do you think killed her?" Ian asked, just out of curiosity.

"Oh, it's not up to me to say."

"What's the most popular opinion on the subject?" Ian asked, trying to push past his reluctance to accuse someone of murder.

Mr. Vinik sighed. "The only one who had any reason to harm her and her baby was the father of that child. He was her boyfriend from college, a rich kid hoping to get richer by marrying a girl with serious money. Didn't want to be saddled with Lorna and her kid so..." he trailed off. The rest was obvious.

"What happened to Lorna's baby?"

"Lorna's grandmother took care of him, but the poor old thing didn't last long. When Lorna's grandmother wasn't well enough to take care of him, the baby was sent to live with relatives somewhere in the Midwest."

Finishing the last of his beer, Mr. Vinik went on his way. Ian was left to mull over what he told him and to wonder why he had been so determined to hear it. Most of what Mr. Vinik said was stuff he sort of knew already but never paid much attention to. It wasn't anything he ever needed to know. Maybe Lorna was haunting her grandmother's house. Maybe that little boy was just playing around. Why did it matter?

After that conversation with the handyman, Ian thought that might be the end of it. He satisfied his curiosity. Now he could drop the whole thing. The weird goings on had nothing to do with him. But every time he passed the back garden of 211, he stopped and stared at the spot by the bench. What he had seen just wouldn't leave him alone.

*

Jacob had been busy with dinner while Toby did his kindergarten homework. Once Toby was done, he went out to play in the garden. Of course he complained when Jacob made him put on his jacket. The evenings were cold now. Leaves were dropping. Jacob felt like he was raking that garden every single day.

Toby had been out there for almost an hour now while the chicken, potatoes, and squash were baking. Seeing that Toby's school things were still on the kitchen table, Jacob decided to call him inside to clear them off and set the table. It would be much easier to do it himself, but parenting wasn't about what was easier.

As he looked for Toby through the kitchen window, Jacob saw him standing by the stone bench. It seemed like he was talking to someone. Toby shook his head then said something

Jacob couldn't hear. From the kitchen window, Jacob had a good view of the garden, and there was no one there.

Stepping outside, Jacob shivered. It was much colder than he expected. The cold made him short of breath and the sound of the wind was too loud in his ears. Actually it wasn't windy at all. He couldn't tell where the sound was coming from, only that it was unnerving. It made his jaw clench.

Jacob called Toby to come inside. He was relieved when they went into the house. It was so much quieter and warmer.

"Weren't you cold out there?" Jacob asked as he watched Toby take off his jacket.

"It's not cold," Toby told him as he hung his jacket on the back of a chair.

"Pick up your stuff and help me set the table," Jacob told him then he asked him about what he had seen. "Who were you talking to out there?"

"The lady," Toby said as he stuffed his things into his book bag.

"A lady? What does she look like?" Jacob asked.

With his chin raised, Toby thought about it. Jacob was half expecting him to say that she was invisible, but Toby simply said, "She has a blue dress."

"Anything else?"

"Like what?" Toby asked.

Jacob picked a piece of information at random. "How old is she?"

"She's a grown-up, but she isn't too old."

"OK. Is she your friend?" Jacob wanted to say imaginary friend, but he didn't think that was the right way to talk to him about it.

"Yeah. I think she's lonely so I tell her what happened at kindergarten and at Ruth's. But she never laughs at anything, not even when it's really funny," Toby said peevishly.

"I see. And what's the lady's name?"

"I asked her, but she never tells me."

"Can't you give her a name?"

Toby seemed puzzled by this suggestion. "Little kids can't give grown-ups names. Can they?"

"But she isn't a regular grown-up," Jacob said though he wasn't sure if Toby realized that.

"I guess not. I'm gonna ask her her name again, but she isn't good at talking," Toby said.

"OK," Jacob said and helped him set the table.

He wanted to know more about this, but he wasn't sure how to ask the right questions. Having imaginary friends wasn't unusual. It was a little strange that Toby hadn't mentioned her before though. Also, he couldn't help but wonder why Toby would have a nameless lady as an imaginary friend.

CHAPTER 3

*Th*ough he couldn't seem to pass up number 211 without staring, Ian didn't have time to obsess about the house that might or might not be haunted. He had more important things to worry about, like his dad's health. To think that at the beginning of his summer break, he didn't even know about his dad's cancer. His father dragged his feet and only told Ian that he wasn't feeling well.

"The doctors are doing tests. But I probably just caught a bug," he said.

The truth was his dad had just been diagnosed with stage 4 lung cancer, but he didn't want Ian to worry.

Ian was in shock for weeks after he found out. His dad always had trouble giving him any kind of bad news. When his parents were splitting up, it was his mom who told him what was happening. This time, Ian had to call her to let her know what was going on with his dad. He barely managed to get the words out. They stuck in his throat and choked him.

The thought that he might lose his dad scared him more than anything ever had before. But as long as there was still even a slim chance, Ian had to get his shit together and help him fight. He drove his dad to his chemo sessions and then took care of him when he got home.

The whole time, his dad never stopped trying to convince

him he was OK, always saying he could manage on his own. He was pushing Ian to go back to school. Looking so pale and weak, he was telling him he was doing fine.

He did it again today. "I'm OK. You really don't need to worry about me. It's not too late for you to go back to school." The man was like a broken record, but he meant well.

"You're a funny guy, Dad. I'm going to make you some ginger lemon tea. But while you're trying to get rid of me, you remember what's waiting for you in that jar." Opening the refrigerator, Ian pointed to the grape jelly jar in the back of the top shelf. It was Mrs. Lincer's homemade spice tea concentrate. Every spice known to man was in there, and the result was vile.

His dad made a face, remembering the taste. He was sitting in the window seat off the kitchen. When it was warmer, he would sit on the back porch. Now the window seat was the closest thing to his favorite spot. He liked the view of the meadow in the back of their house.

While he made the tea, Ian thought that's what his father was looking at. Then he realized his dad was checking out his own reflection in the glass. As long as Ian could remember, his dad's hair had always been thin. Chemo had left him with so little, he just shaved it all off.

"I think I look better with no hair. Sort of like Vin Diesel, right?" his dad said.

"Right this minute, I can't even tell you apart. I was just asking myself, 'Should I make an extra cup of tea for Vin Diesel or what?' Dad, you're blowing my mind. It's like you're twins."

His dad grinned at him. He was trying so hard to keep up his own spirits and Ian's too. The least he could do was return the favor.

As his dad dozed off, Ian straightened up a little around the house. His dad was never good at picking up after himself, and now he didn't have the energy. Looking around for what needed to be done, Ian took in the familiar, old place.

The house was Dad's family home going back several generations. He was really attached to it and its history. That was no wonder. Dad was a professional history buff. The Civil War was his specialty. Until he got sick, he had made a living writing books about it and giving lectures. He often took Ian with him on his research trips and lecture tours. Then it was back home to write his heart out.

Ian didn't share his passion for writing, history, or even the house where he grew up. During his childhood, the house was an obstacle course of old furniture with a banister he wasn't allowed to slide down, but he did anyway. But being so old, it was no surprise that the house was a little gloomy. That's how it seemed to Ian anyway, especially after his mom moved away. He was in high school then and splitting his time between his dad's place and his mom's. The contrast between their houses didn't do his dad's house any favors.

For the last two years, Ian had spent most of his time away at school. It was weird to be back here. Not just at the house though. Inside the house and for miles around, all the way into Blystone, Ian had scattered bits and pieces of his childhood.

The pieces of his childhood that obsessed him right now had to do with that house, number 211. As he was growing up, he remembered it sitting abandoned, surrounded by an overgrown yard. With its gates chained shut, it called to any adventurous boy or girl to jump the fence if they dared.

Ian had done it only once. What happened after he went over the fence was unclear to him. The garden was cool and dark. The trees and bushes had grown big. Rising high above an eight-year-old boy's head, they smothered the sunlight.

But it couldn't have been as dark and cold as he

remembered. Wasn't it summer? And why couldn't he breathe? Ian tried to remember, but it was murky. He hit a blank wall when he tried to focus on the memory. He did remember running away from there, scared, breathless, not stopping until he got home.

CHAPTER 4

By the time he ran into the father and son who lived at number 211, Ian had already heard a few things about them. The father had moved there for work. He was some kind of supervisor at the HCL Testing Service Lab out toward Lambton. The kid went to the local kindergarten and to daycare at Ruth Miller's.

This was another day when Ian roamed the town and the countryside, trying to clear his head of all his worries about his dad. He slept better if he did that. Afternoons were a good time. That's when his father rested quietly.

On his aimless walk through town, Ian turned a corner and almost collided with the father and his little boy in front of Ruth's front gate. It looked like they had just come out from the daycare place.

"Oh, you guys," Ian said. He turned his eyes from the blond kid to the guy he had only seen from a distance until now. Up close, he was kind of stunning. His face was chiseled. His eyes were light blue, catching flashes of gold from the afternoon sun.

Ian extended his hand for a handshake. "Hi. I'm Ian Warwick. I live up the road. And you're Jake Conroy, right?"

"It's Jacob," he corrected him, shaking his hand.

"Oh. Sorry."

"I'm Toby," his son said, looking up at Ian, not wanting to be left out.

"Nice to meet you, Tony," Ian said.

Toby made a face at him. "He got my name wrong too," he complained to his dad.

"I think he's just kidding around," Jacob told him with a smile.

"A joke? Good one!" Toby told Ian.

Ian gave him a wink. He decided to walk along with them as they went toward their house. Toby walked ahead, exploring the bushes, and poking into hedges. He was a little boy on a mission.

"He's looking for frogs and grasshoppers, anything that jumps. But they're all gone," Jacob told him. He looked at his son and smiled.

The two of them didn't look very much alike except for the eyes. Their eyes were exactly the same. That prompted Ian to ask, "How did you get him?"

Jacob grimaced at him. "Get him?"

"You're gay, aren't you? Were you married once or something? To a woman, I mean."

Jacob didn't confirm he was gay, but he looked at Ian like he was wondering how he knew. He did answer his question about his son. "I had him with the help of in vitro and a surrogate."

"I could tell he was yours because of the eyes," Ian said. He wondered how far that went. What did Jacob Conroy see when his kid talked to invisible people in the back garden?

"And do you live here?" Jacob asked, maybe just to stop Ian from staring at him.

"Not really. I'm taking a year off from school to be with my dad. He's sick. Lung cancer."

"I'm sorry."

"I don't need condolences. He'll beat it. Or I hope he will.

18

He was never good about taking care of himself. He ignored his health no matter how bad he felt. By the time he was diagnosed, his cancer had spread."

"It's good of you to stay here and be with him."

"I know where I need to be, but my dad keeps trying to send me back to school. I'm not going anywhere. We do have help. Mrs. Astor comes by to check on him. She's a retired nurse. We're lucky she lives just down the road. Our house is outside of town so we don't exactly have next door neighbors." Ian rattled on, but Jacob didn't seem to mind.

"One of those old houses you can see far back from the road?" Jacob said.

"That's us. If you ever want to drop in just look for the name Warwick on the mailbox," Ian said with a grin. And there he was, flirting.

Jacob gave him a wry look, not exactly warning him off but close.

*

When he first arrived in town, Jacob only had a few days before he started his job. He had the kindergarten sorted out, but he had to go and check out the daycare place. Toby loved it at first sight. Not the place so much as the two dogs that came to greet them. While Toby played with the dogs, Ruth, the owner of the small daycare center, told Jacob, "It's not me that babysits them. It's the dogs."

That didn't give Jacob a ton of confidence, but the place had a great reputation and the dogs were two sweet, little terriers. Toby loved them already. It turned out that they really were useful when it came to watching the kids. The dogs were trained to bark if the kids went anywhere near the gate.

That wasn't the way a daycare was supposed to be run, but

in a small town, Jacob figured he would have to put up with a few small town quirks. At least Toby liked it there, and that was the main thing. After work, when he walked to Ruth's to pick up his son, Jacob got to see it for himself. He always hung back for a few minutes and watched Toby playing with the other kids. He was a happy boy.

Today was supposed to be another routine day of work then picking up Toby from daycare and going home. But then Jacob's day hit a snag and now nothing was going the way it was supposed to. First he couldn't remember how to unlock his phone because someone's dark blue eyes looked too long into his. With those eyes on him, it was impossible to remember his own name. Jacob stood just inside his front door, trying to remember a pattern he used countless times a day. Finally he got it, and managed not to lock himself out of his phone.

Making dinner turned into a major challenge too. He spent about half an hour looking for the ground beef in the fridge and the freezer. Finally he realized he never bought it. That wouldn't have happened if he wasn't imagining what Ian might smell like. He wore a black pea coat, and the space between his collar and his neck was irresistible. Jacob could just bury his face there and breathe him in forever.

After he settled for ground turkey, he burned the meatballs and filled the house with a terrible stench. He had to serve plain spaghetti and sauce. Being a big meatball fan, Toby was not happy with him.

And it was all because Jacob had met that intense young guy on the walk home. Scruffy, dark brown hair, dark blue eyes, tall and wiry, and possibly gay – almost certainly gay – he was definitely bad news. Why did he have such a strong effect on him?

Jacob had been hoping to find a gay guy nearby, but

someone like that was not what he had in mind. That guy couldn't be more than twenty, and Jacob was looking for someone who wanted to get serious. After just one quick conversation, this guy was already causing him trouble.

OK, maybe it wasn't fair to blame him for his own overactive imagination. Maybe he just needed to get laid. At this point, he'd kill for a hand job. But not from him. Damn it. Too late.

Now he was thinking about that guy's hand wrapped around his cock. Bet his grip would be loose at first then slow and tight while his eyes burned into him like blowtorches. Blow. Why settle for a hand job? His mouth would be even better. Wide and expressive, it would feel amazing on his cock.

And this is how meatballs get burned. Balls. Don't think about balls. Jacob looked down at his plate of plain spaghetti then over at the trashcan full of ruined dinner. He needed to get a grip. Grip. No. A tight grip on his cock. No and no. Why was the English language booby trapped. Good thing the word booby did nothing for him at all.

"No meatball sandwiches for lunch," Toby said as Jacob started to clear the table.

"Sorry," Jacob told him. "I'll try again tomorrow. Maybe we'll have meatball sandwiches for dinner."

"Yes. Try to do a good job and not mess up again," Toby instructed him. Then he told him a story, or at least a series of words.

When he came from daycare, Toby was always full of stories. They spilled out of him in a high pitched torrent broken up by laughter. Jacob could never get more than half of what he was talking about. Today, Jacob had no hope of making sense of any of it. How could meeting some random guy scramble his brain like this?

"Can I go and play outside?" Toby asked.

Jacob had no reason to say no, but he hesitated. "Help me with dishes and we'll go together. We can kick the soccer ball around. We don't want you to forget how to play," Jacob told him.

Toby used to play soccer at his preschool. His kindergarten here wasn't much into soccer. That made soccer their special father son activity. But today Jacob had only used it as an excuse. Since he had seen Toby talking to his imaginary friend out there, leaving him alone in the garden made him uneasy.

CHAPTER 5

" Why are you smiling?" his dad asked him as Ian was cleaning up after breakfast.

Ian straightened with plates in his hand. "I didn't realize I was," he told him.

His dad gave him a knowing smile. While sticking dishes in the dishwasher, Ian noticed how little his dad ate off his plate. That's what should be on his mind. Instead, Ian was picturing the exact line of Jacob's mouth, then tracing over it with his fingertip, then with his tongue.

Seeing Jacob in person reminded Ian what he had been missing for months. How good was the body under those conservative clothes? Ian was dying to find out. Jacob looked trim. Ian saw hints of a hard body with good definition. That body would feel so good pressed up against him, on top of him, pounding into him.

If only he could get him out of those clothes and do a thorough inspection. To make absolutely sure, his hands wouldn't be enough. Ian would need to let his lips trace every contour, every dip around a muscle, and every vein. His teeth might need to get into the action, and his tongue would have to taste every inch.

Enough of that. If he kept that up while doing dishes, he wouldn't need to worry about an errant smile on his face. The problem would be further south and a lot more embarrassing. He didn't expect that meeting a guy who wasn't even his type would have such a strong impact.

Plus meeting Jacob and his son hadn't done a thing to ease Ian's obsession with the weird stuff that went on over at their house. Whenever he walked that way, he couldn't pass by without lingering at their back gate and trying to catch sight of something that wasn't there.

Today was no different. While his father dozed, Ian had gone into town. Once he was at the edge of Jacob's yard, he paused and stared toward the back wall of the garden. Since that day when he first saw Toby talking to no one, Ian hadn't stopped questioning what it was that he had seen. No matter how hard he looked, the bench, the wall, the shadows cast by the trees didn't give him any answers.

Just before moving on, he saw something out of the corner of his eye. He looked back. There was a patch of blue above the garden bench. Ian tried hard to convince himself that it was just some blue paint on the wall. Maybe the whitewashing had chipped away. But that wasn't it. The patch of blue wasn't paint, and now it was spreading.

Ian couldn't help himself. He had to get closer. Letting himself in by the back gate, he went into Jacob's yard. He walked toward the bench slowly. His feet were heavy. They dragged and his breath grew short.

As he got closer, he watched the shimmer of blue grow bigger. It was like someone was painting a picture in midair, but it was smeared. As a rushing noise filled his ears, Ian stared at the shape that was forming right in front of him. He stared like his life depended on it. Maybe it did. Taking each breath had become a huge effort. His chest felt tight, not leaving enough room for his lungs to take in air or for his heart to beat.

His hands felt cold and numb. A chill spread up his arms

24

then reached deep inside him. A tremor in his bones made it up to his stiff jaw and made his teeth chatter. But he still kept looking. Even as he felt his whole body shake and he was gasping for breath, he wanted to see the shape that was slowly being revealed.

Then just as he was sure it was a woman, the noise in his ears became unbearably loud. It almost sounded like words, but they were painfully loud and incomprehensible. Then suddenly, the shape was gone and he could breathe again. He shivered, but the extreme chill was leaving his body.

He stood there for a while and stared, breathing hard. There was nothing to see. Weak, autumn sunlight came down filtered between branches and played over the wall. A few yellow leaves tumbled across the lawn. It was just a peaceful day in autumn, and Ian was trespassing.

After his experience in the garden, Ian couldn't stop thinking about the terrible feeling that gripped him during the encounter. He couldn't explain what happened, but it made him worry about that little boy. He couldn't ignore this. Even if he ended up sounding like a nut job, he had to talk to Jacob. He didn't know what he would say to him, but somehow he had to let him know to keep an eye on Toby.

Determined to make a fool of himself, Ian dropped by next Sunday. It was a sunny day. Patches of midmorning sunshine among all the greens and yellows made the garden cheerful. He was in luck. Toby and Jacob were in their back garden, enjoying the nice day. Or one of them was. Jacob was raking leaves, and Toby was helping him by kicking some leaves around.

Toby was the first to notice Ian lurking behind the fence. He pointed him out to his father.

"It's that guy who got our names wrong," Toby said.

Jacob waved at him and Toby ran over to Ian.

"You guys look busy," Ian said.

"We're raking leaves. Dad hates leaves," Toby informed him.

"I don't hate them. I hate raking them," Jacob grumbled.

"In that case, don't look up," Ian told him. There were plenty of leaves left on the branches above them. "Lots more where those came from."

"You want to come over for lunch?" Jacob asked him. "It's just sandwiches, turkey and swiss."

"Sounds good," Ian said and went in through the back gate. Being in that garden again, he couldn't help but think back to the last time he was there. But after a few steps, that thought was driven right out of his head. He was standing face to face with Jacob, and his heart was pounding harder than it ever had in his life.

Ian wanted to chalk that up to not having seen many attractive guys lately, not in the flesh anyway. But the feeling on seeing Jacob up close had the intensity of a punch. It triggered such overwhelming desire. It stole his breath away. Ian tried to shake it off. This was no time for that.

Accompanying Jacob and Toby as they went into the kitchen, Ian was surprised he got invited over. He expected to have to lure Jacob somewhere so they would have a chance to talk. This might make it easier. He just had to wait for an opportunity.

From the kitchen, Ian could see a little bit of their house. It had a cottage feel to it. The décor was a little stuffy but not as bad as his dad's house. Overall it was cozy with Toby marking his territory with toys everywhere.

Turning his attention back to the kitchen, Ian offered to help with lunch, but Toby had that covered. As his father got plates for sandwiches, Toby got the ingredients together. He was handing Jacob gag ingredients like grape jelly and pancake syrup and giggling. When Toby handed his dad a bottle of ketchup, Ian was sure that was a joke too. But it wasn't. Jacob put some on the smallest of the three sandwiches.

"Ketchup on turkey? That can't be right," Ian said.

"I like ketchup," Toby told him.

"Not on turkey," Ian said.

"Yes," Toby insisted. Seeing his father close the ketchup bottle, Toby said, "More."

Jacob indulged him and put a little more while Ian shook his head.

"That's a crime."

With a plate and a drink in hand, the three of them went outside to eat. The breeze was cool. Coming down between thinning branches, sunshine warmed them where they sat at the outdoor table. Patches of sunlight moved as the tree branches swayed in the breeze. Like a cat, Toby kept trying to swat them. Finished with his sandwich first, he ran off to play.

After a while, Ian noticed that he was digging and then taking something from his pocket. "What's he doing?"

"I told him how squirrels bury nuts for the winter so he's helping them out. He's burying peanuts," Jacob told him.

"Peanuts? He's a sweet kid," Ian said then he turned his attention back to Jacob.

All through lunch, Ian had been glancing toward the far side of the garden where the bench was. It surprised him to catch Jacob doing the same thing.

"How come you kept looking over there?" Ian asked. He knew why his own eyes strayed that way every few minutes. Now he wondered if Jacob had seen something too.

"Toby has an imaginary friend, I guess. He talks to her. He says she comes from over there."

If that was his explanation for what was happening, it was no reason to wear such a heavy frown.

"It worries you," Ian said. It was obvious that it did.

Jacob nodded. "I've seen him talk to her a few times now. It looks strange, and the way he describes her sounds strange too."

"What did he say his friend looks like?" Ian asked, maybe a little too eagerly.

Jacob didn't seem to notice his strong interest. He told Ian, "He said his friend is a lady. I didn't get much more than that. Getting a description out of a five-year-old isn't easy. He did say that she was a grown-up and that she was wearing a blue dress."

Hearing that, Ian held his breath. He tried not to act weird and asked, "What bothers you about it?"

"It's strange. Maybe I'm just stereotyping, but why would a five-year-old boy have a 'lady' as his imaginary friend and not a brontosaurus or something?"

"You think it's something else?"

"I... I don't know. I just know it worries me, but maybe it shouldn't," Jacob said with a shrug.

"You think it might be a ghost?" Ian blurted out. He knew when he started this that there was no way he wouldn't end up sounding like a lunatic. But he just couldn't let Jacob dismiss what was happening because it worried him too.

Jacob turned to him with a suspicious look. "Why did you say that?"

"No reason." Ian said. He was a little flustered now that Jacob was looking at him so sharply with those incredible blue eyes.

"Really? Have you ever seen a ghost?" Jacob asked him. His skeptical tone was daring him to say yes.

"Why? Have you?" Ian said, not wanting to stick his neck out. But then he had to confess. Afraid that Jacob was going to tell him to just get the fuck out, Ian was inching toward the truth. "I might have seen something. Maybe even right here."

"If you saw something, I want to know. This is about my

kid," Jacob demanded sternly.

"I saw something over there." Ian pointed toward the back wall. "Just a blue shape that disappeared."

"That doesn't mean anything. It could have been just a trick of the light." They both looked at the shapes that the sunshine made on the wall as it came down between the yellowing leaves.

"It looked like a woman in a blue dress and it gave me a chill."

"Weather is getting cold," Jacob said, deadpan.

"Not that kind of chill."

"I did feel it's colder out here than it should be sometimes. Usually when Toby is talking with his friend. He doesn't seem to feel it though," Jacob said, looking worried again.

Ian was relieved that Jacob wasn't calling him crazy. Maybe they might even figure this out, but first he wanted to know more about what Jacob experienced. "Did you ever hear anything?"

"Maybe," Jacob said. He wasn't eager to share, but then he admitted, "There was a rushing sound. It stopped suddenly, but that could have been anything."

"Like a plane going overhead? And maybe your back yard gets as cold as the Arctic for a perfectly logical reason. Or you might have sensed the presence of the same ghost your son is seeing," Ian said.

Jacob wasn't going to accept that explanation so easily. "Or maybe I'm making too much out of a chill in the air and an unexplained noise or two."

"Or maybe you're just crazy," Ian threw in.

"Maybe we're both crazy," Jacob told him with a wry look. Then he got serious. "I would rather think I was crazy than believe that Toby is talking to a ghost."

Ian took a deep breath. "OK, but what if I tell you that I think I know who this lady is?"

"Who?" Jacob said though he didn't necessarily want to hear the answer.

Ian told him anyway. "There was a girl who lived here, in this house. Her name was Lorna Hayes. That was around twenty years ago."

"She didn't die here, did she?" It was clear he dreaded a yes.

"No. She was killed right up the road, where that roadside memorial is. She was pregnant, and she lived just long enough to give birth to a baby. I think that might be why she's fixated on your son."

"You think Toby is seeing this Lorna Hayes? How can this even be real?" Jacob said, dismayed.

Ian didn't have all the answers. "I believe what I see. And I kind of saw her. Just for a second. She was wearing a blue dress just like Toby said."

Jacob was shaking his head.

"You told me you felt weird things too," Ian told him.

"But to believe..."

Without waiting for him to say how crazy this was, Ian told him what else he knew. "I think she's been here since she died. Her grandmother said she saw her. That was right after she was killed. Then more recently, the handyman that the real-estate office hired to fix up the place saw and heard something while he was working here."

Jacob opened his mouth to speak, but just then Toby came running back. He had been playing on the side of the house and peering anxiously toward the front.

"When is Franny coming?" he asked his dad.

"In a few minutes," Jacob told him after he checked his phone. He then turned to Ian. "He's going with her and her kids to visit some chickens she's feeding."

"Chickens are funny," Toby said.

A few minutes later, Franny James was there with her SUV full of kids.

"Kids are really into chickens, huh," Ian said seeing them all excited as Toby climbed in.

"I think they just like to get together and drive Fran crazy. She looked like she aged ten years when she brought the kids back from an outing last week. That brave, selfless woman," Jacob said. It was clear that he did not envy her.

Once they saw Toby off, he and Jacob walked around the side of the house and returned to the back garden. Ian was thinking that maybe he should go, but he really didn't want to.

Jacob was thoughtful, almost brooding. It was a sexy look on him. Ian just wanted to stare at his chiseled features and into his light blue eyes.

That was probably why he made his proposition. "Want to see if we can catch sight of that ghost?"

"You mean stand around in my back yard, feeling like idiots and then what? Call Lorna Hayes' name three times?"

Ian hadn't thought of that. "That's something we could try."

"Let's not. I feel stupid enough just considering the possibility that she is real."

"And what do you feel when it's deathly cold out here and you hear a rushing noise that gets louder and louder in your ears?" Ian shivered at the thought.

Jacob did too but he tried not to let it show. Ian didn't blame him for fighting the idea. He knew that this was a bigger deal to him. This was about his kid. Ian just wished that he could do something to help, or at least that he could say something to make him feel better.

For now they just stood around in the back yard, keeping an eye on that back wall. Nothing happened. The garden stayed pleasantly cool and sunny. The only noises were perfectly natural – leaves shushing in the breeze and a lonely bird singing somewhere high above.

Trina Solet

"It's crazy to think that when you decide to see a ghost, one will appear," Jacob said.

"Who knows? But if she does show, this time we'll both see her, and I'll feel a tiny bit less crazy."

"Whatever I can do to make you feel better," Jacob said offhandedly.

Ian narrowed his eyes at him. "A guy like you shouldn't make an offer like that."

"Did I make an offer? I think you might be hearing things again. And what do you mean a guy like me?"

"Hot but all buttoned up, repressed and ready to explode," Ian summed up.

"You're dangerously low on credibility and losing more by the second," Jacob said. "How did you know I was gay anyway?"

"You've been dying to ask me that, haven't you?" Ian said, then he told him how he gave himself away. "As soon as you set eyes on me, you scoped me out from head to toe. That look was just short of a grope. Then you did a little 'Oh, yeah, I'd do him.'"

"I didn't do any of that," Jacob claimed.

"You did all of it. And I appreciate the compliment."

"And are you out around here?" Jacob asked him in a let's change the subject tone.

"I am at home, but I'm not sure if word has gotten around. I came out to my dad just before I went off to college. I said, 'Dad, I'm gay. That OK?' And he said, 'You're OK with me no matter what.'"

"And how is he doing?" Jacob asked more seriously.

"The chemo isn't exactly kicking the cancer's ass. Mainly it's been keeping him from getting worse. He has some bad days, but he doesn't get down too much."

"That's probably thanks to you."

"You think?"

"As a father, I'm absolutely sure of it."

Damn, he was sexy even when he had that fond, fatherly look on his face. This guy was going to drive him crazy. Ian decided to take a step or two away from him before he jumped him and got himself kicked to the curb.

Jacob leaned on the brick wall of the house while Ian paced back and forth in front of him. At the moment, it wasn't the ghost that had Ian all wound up. Being alone with Jacob was getting to him.

Looking at Jacob, you would think he was a hundred percent at ease. But his pose only seemed relaxed. There was something about him coiled tight. Just under the surface lurked something hot and alive, a muscular beast poised to strike.

Though he had been watching him out of the corner of his eye, when he did strike, it was a shock. Jacob moved fast. He grabbed Ian's arm to pull him around to face him. For a moment, Ian was looking at his incredible blue eyes, then the next moment he was being swung around and pushed up against the wall. His legs were bent, braced for the impact of Jacob's body as he slammed into him.

The wall was hard against the back of his head, and Jacob's mouth was stealing his breath. His tongue was lapping at Ian's. Ian was pushed and pulled and torn apart by the force of that kiss. Pinned to the wall by Jacob's brutal grip on his shoulders, Ian moaned. Jacob's tongue thrust into his mouth. Rough bricks on one side, Jacob's rock hard body on the other, Ian was lost.

While Jacob's mouth was rough and urgent on his, Ian's whole body throbbed. Jacob was grinding into him like he wanted to crush him. Their erections rubbed together through two sets of jeans. That only meant that they had to push harder. Didn't matter if it hurt as long as he could feel the hardness of Jacob's cock. It was digging into him, almost through him while Jacob's mouth smothered him sweetly.

Jacob moaned then wrenched himself away with an angry grunt. That was another good look on Jacob. They stood there glaring at each other with unsatisfied lust like two halves of one thing being torn apart. Panting, Jacob calmed down a little and seemed to be wondering what he had done.

"Sorry, got carried away," he said to Ian.

"You only surprised yourself. I knew you were an animal ready to pounce," Ian said.

He was gasping for breath as he spoke. That wasn't the kind of kiss you could breathe through. It was the kind of kiss that slays you. Even as he was trying to recover from it, Ian had a suspicion that he never would.

Jacob had woken up a restless ache inside him. Now he was trying to shrug it off, act casual again. Even if he did send Ian home right after, what he had done was as good as a promise. Ian was counting on him to lose control again.

CHAPTER 6

After Ian left, Jacob sobered only enough to curse himself for what he did, not enough to want to take it back. He did wonder what the hell got into him. He had never made such a violent move on a guy.

But it wasn't a passing thing. He wanted Ian that much even now. The way Ian welcomed him into his arms told him that it was mutual. It was as if he had been waiting for Jacob to do just that, and every inch of him was ready for his forceful kiss and every second of their hard grinding.

Now Jacob's need for him was so heightened, it made him want to scream. That overwhelming need had driven him into Ian. It was like he wanted to break them both. He wanted to shatter this thing between them with the hardest kiss he had ever planted on anyone.

In Ian's absence, Jacob waited for the feeling to pass, but it didn't. He was just as desperate for Ian as he had been when he slammed him into that brick wall and crashed into him. With every second, the feeling grew and became more and more a part of him.

Luckily, a few days passed before Jacob saw Ian again. Another good thing was that Toby was there to chaperone this time. He and Toby were out taking a walk through the fields on the outskirts of town. There wasn't much to see around there, but every few steps Toby found something to interest him.

Toby was looking at the ground and Jacob was looking around when he spotted Ian. He was on the other side of the road from them. Jacob waved him over.

"It looks like it might rain. You guys are brave," Ian said as he came up to him.

Jacob had noticed that the sky was mostly gray. "We're exploring the countryside."

"And what's Toby up to?" Ian asked.

Toby was a few yards away, absorbed in what he was doing. He didn't even notice Ian, maybe because he wasn't a small, creepy crawly thing.

"He found an empty snail shell. He thinks there's a snail around here that's missing his shell. I didn't have the heart to tell him that the snail was dead." Jacob sighed then turned from Toby to Ian. "Speaking of the dead. I talked to Toby some more about his friend, and he told me something interesting. He has only ever seen her in the back garden, never inside the house."

"Really?" Ian was surprised. "That's good, I guess. But she lived there for years. Why wouldn't she show up inside too?" he wondered.

"Toby told me it's because 'Grandma is sleeping.'"

"Lorna's grandmother? That keeps her out of the house?"

Jacob shrugged. "That's what Toby said."

"I know Lorna's grandmother died soon after she did," Ian said with a thoughtful frown.

"Since Toby said she was sleeping, could she have died in the house?" Jacob asked.

"I don't know, but I'll ask around," Ian said. "Does that mean that you're finally a hundred percent sold on this ghost theory?"

"Not even fifty percent," Jacob said, turning away.

"You would be if you saw her," Ian predicted.

"I'd rather not."

Jacob decided it was time to distract Toby from his futile search. He called out to him, "Hey, Toby, look who joined us."

Toby raised his head and ran over eagerly. "Want to help me find a snail?" he asked Ian.

Knowing that was hopeless, Ian said, "How about if we do something else? Did you go up to the bridge yet?"

Toby shook his head.

"Then let's go there together," Ian suggested.

They cut across the field until they came to an old stone bridge that curved over a thin stream. On either side of the bridge there was a dirt road. Getting onto the road, they crossed to the middle of the bridge. Jacob picked up Toby so he could look down over the side, not that there was much to see. The stream was only a few feet wide. Walking the rest of the way over the bridge, they circled around to a path that led down to the streambed.

"The stream is bigger in the spring and summer. Now we can jump right over it," Ian said.

"No. Not you," Jacob warned Toby who looked ready to try it.

"Can I go fishing?" Toby asked as they stood right on the edge of the stream.

"Sure, why not?" Jacob told him though he saw no sign of any fish.

Toby ran around until he found a stick. He waved it in the air triumphantly then stuck it into the water.

"That's how he goes fishing?" Ian said.

Jacob shrugged. "Once I learn how to fish, I'll get around to teaching him."

"My dad taught me. He was terrible at it and so am I," Ian

said with a proud smile.

Looking at him, Jacob got wistful. Maybe years from now, Toby would sound like that when he talked about what Jacob taught him. He could only hope.

With Toby busy fishing, the two of them walked a few steps away to stand right under the bridge. They both looked up at its underside. Jacob could see plants growing in the cracks between the stones.

"A lot of them have dried up, but it's all green in the summer. Like some upside down jungle," Ian said. "There are all sorts of neat things around here. I wouldn't mind showing Toby all the cool spots I discovered as a kid. I'll be saving him a ton of legwork."

"Where's the fun in that?" Jacob asked and looked back at Toby, who was peering expectantly at the water. Jacob wondered what he thought was going to happen.

When Jacob turned he noticed Ian eyeing him. "I can't see you letting him run around loose the way I did."

"You still think I'm some stick in the mud."

Ian nodded then he stepped closer. "But you can always prove me wrong."

In his corduroy jacket, hair messy from the wind, skin ruddy from the cool air, Ian was so vivid and somehow too real. Jacob felt like he had never seen anything as clearly as he saw him at that moment.

He was close enough for Jacob to breathe him in. A few inches forward and he could be kissing him, reaching under his jacket and running his hands all over him. Jacob didn't go that far, but he did let Ian place his hands on his chest.

"I'm dying to see what you look like with all this off." Ian's eyes became sharp like they would slice through Jacob's clothes.

He then looked up from Jacob's chest to his eyes. He tilted his head up and parted his lips slightly – a dare Jacob couldn't pass up. His gaze sinking into Ian's dark blue eyes, he leaned down and only let his lips brush over his. Then he straightened while Ian shook his head at him and smiled ruefully.

The touch of their lips took only a second, but Toby wasn't far. He just had to stop poking around in the stream, turn around, and he would see... What? His father acting like an idiot, going crazy for a young guy who filled his head with weird ideas and his heart with feelings he couldn't resist.

There was no future with Ian. This couldn't happen, but it was happening anyway. He should have never let their lips touch. Now their heads were tilting, mouths lining up, lips parting. They both took one last breath then held it.

When it seemed like a sure thing that what happened before would happen again, Toby saved Jacob from himself. He picked that moment to jump up and run over to them.

"I didn't catch any fish," he announced but he didn't seem unhappy about it.

With a tiny gasp he looked up at the sky. Birds were swooping overhead, a whole flock of them probably on their way south. Toby watched them entranced. There were so many things in this world to interest him, why did he have to see the things of that other world?

That night after dinner, Toby was watching TV, and Jacob was clearing up in the kitchen. What he was really doing was thinking about Ian. He should be putting him out of his head. Or at least he should leave thoughts of him for jerking off. There was no reason to think about him constantly.

With Toby to worry about, how could he even consider an insane infatuation with a college kid? The answer came to him as he replayed their kiss and let Ian's eyes dance over him mischievously. He craved Ian under him and next to him. He wanted to fuck him, but he also wanted him in this kitchen right now even if all he did was talk about ghosts.

Jacob groaned at his own stupidity and grabbed the bag of garbage from the kitchen. He tied it off and took it out. Maybe some cold air in his lungs would help clear his head.

He dumped the bag in the garbage can on the side of the house and looked up. The dark blue sky reminded him of Ian's eyes. Well, this wasn't working. He could feel the shape of his mouth and its taste. He could hear his voice, low and husky.

Jacob took a deep breath of cool, night air. It was bracing out there, but Ian was still lingering on his mind, giving him a teasing smile. That smile was begging for a hard kiss to wipe it off.

Distracted, Jacob wandered the garden. Suddenly he noticed that he had walked toward the stone bench without realizing it. He stopped a few feet away from it.

Staring ahead of him, he wasn't sure if he was hoping to see something or not to see it. For Toby's sake, he needed to try and confirm if this was real. But was standing there and staring really hard supposed to accomplish that?

Feeling stupid, Jacob was ready to head inside when he suddenly felt very cold. As his ears filled with the rushing noise he recognized, his chest felt painfully tight. Every breath he took was a struggle like the air was too thick to breathe. His vision was turning black. Then he saw it. A bright spot bloomed in the thickening darkness.

As he stared, a shape slowly formed in midair – a woman's hand. It was hazy as if he couldn't focus on it properly. The bright spot expanded into a patch of blue vaguely resembling a woman whose face was in shadow.

Looking at the shape, Jacob felt as if there was something wrong with his vision, but that wasn't it. The image was winking in and out rapidly. It made him feel dizzy.

The noise that still flooded his ears resolved into something like garbled speech. It was too loud but incomprehensible. If she wanted to tell him something, he couldn't understand her.

"What do you want with my son?" he choked out.

In response, there was only more noise. The pressure in his head and in his lungs was so intense, he thought he might pass out. But just as he thought he was reaching his limit, it all stopped.

Jacob stared around him. The streetlight lit up the space, showing only the things that should be there. It was just an ordinary garden that needed raking again.

Jacob breathed easier, but his heart was still beating too fast and hard. This was his proof about what was happening, but the unsettling experience left him with more unanswered questions than answers. It did seem like she tried to speak to him, but he just couldn't understand her. Even without getting any answers from her, Jacob now knew what had to be done.

CHAPTER 7

It wasn't hard to find out the information about the death of Lorna's grandmother. It was common knowledge among the older residents of Blystone. Heading over to Jacob's house the next day, Ian was eager to share what he had found out. It was time for Jacob to head out to work so he hurried to catch him. His car was still there, so he had to be home. Ian went up to his door and knocked.

Every time he saw Jacob, it hit him how gorgeous the man was. Seeing him as he opened the door took his breath away again, but he couldn't dwell on that. Standing on his doorstep, he started speaking before Jacob had a chance to greet him.

"You were right. Lorna's grandmother did die in this house. She died in her sleep. And good morning," he added. "I was wondering if she might be a ghost too? Has Toby ever seen her?"

Instead of inviting Ian in, Jacob stepped out and locked the door. "I already asked him if this lady was the only person he ever saw who wasn't always there. I wasn't sure how to put it. He said she was the only one," Jacob said.

"Would he know the difference between seeing a living person and a dead one? Does he even realize Lorna is dead?" Ian wondered as he walked Jacob to his car.

Jacob shook his head. Ian could tell that he was frustrated by everything he didn't know about what was happening to his little boy. But Ian didn't realize how far things had gone until Jacob told him what he was planning.

"I can't risk staying here. I've decided to move out of the house. I can't have Toby here with what's happening."

Ian grabbed his arm as if Jacob was going to run away right then. "Wait. What's changed?"

Jacob frowned deeply as he turned toward him. "I saw her. But it wasn't so much seeing her. She wasn't very distinct. It was the feeling. I couldn't breathe. I felt paralyzed and cold. The feeling was so debilitating."

"But Toby doesn't experience any of that, does he?" Ian asked.

"No. I asked him, and he doesn't. But this is so much more real to me now. I need to get him away from here."

"Maybe kids have a more natural connection than adults," Ian said, as he wondered why Toby seemed to have such a different experience.

"Maybe, but that doesn't matter now. I need Toby to be safe," Jacob said firmly.

"Are there any houses available around here?" Ian tried to think of places they might rent. He didn't want Jacob and Toby to have to move too far away.

"We aren't staying in Blystone," Jacob told him. "Anywhere in town or in the area would be too close. My sister has an apartment in Lambton. She has pretty much moved in with her boyfriend. She said we can stay at her place."

"I didn't realize you were moving so far," Ian said.

"It's not that far. It's only a little further from my work. But I'm sorry to have to take Toby out of kindergarten and daycare here. It's so disruptive."

"Damn. When will you be leaving?"

"Tomorrow," Jacob said. He looked just as unhappy about it as Ian felt.

"So soon?"

"I would be out of here today if I could." Jacob's face was grim.

"OK. I'll stop by to see you off," Ian told him and then he let him go to work.

As Jacob drove away, Ian just stood there. He wanted to curse and scream. He looked at Jacob's house and then past it to the garden in the back. If he could only figure this out, Jacob and Toby wouldn't need to leave. What the hell did that dead woman want?

Next day Ian texted with Jacob and found out he would be at the house until the afternoon. He dropped by around noon, and Jacob let him in. As soon as he stepped inside, Ian could see packed bags waiting by the door. A few other things were in a box. That was it for now, but Ian figured that eventually they would pack up everything and be gone for good. It made him unbearably sad.

"I took today off. I'll be picking up Toby from kindergarten and we'll be going to Lambton from there," Jacob told him as they went through to the kitchen.

"Can I come with you to see you both off?"

"Sounds good. Did you have lunch? I can't eat but if you want something..."

"No. I'm fine." Ian didn't have much of an appetite under the circumstances. He just wanted to spend as much time with Jacob as he could. "I'll keep you company until it's time to go. You need help with anything?"

"I'm just getting a few things ready," Jacob said pointing to a box that held plates and cups that had cartoon characters on them as well as some toys. "I thought it would be better to do this while Toby was in kindergarten. I want him to spend as little time here as possible so I'm packing for both of us. God help me when I forget to pack some crucial toy." Jacob then got some snacks from the cupboard and stuck them in a different box.

"You'll be back for the rest of your stuff, right?" Ian didn't want to accept that this was the last time he would be seeing him.

"Maybe not. I might just hire movers. I need to find some place more permanent than my sister's apartment though."

"I'm really sorry this happened," Ian said, not hiding how upset he was.

"Me too."

Ian looked at him and wondered if he could possibly regret leaving for the same reason he did. "You haven't been here long enough to miss the place." Ian pointed around, but Jacob only looked at him. It was a sad, intense stare that made him shiver.

"We barely got to know each other," Jacob said, his voice hushed and raw.

That was unexpected. Ian was caught so off guard, he couldn't say anything back though he felt the same way. Jacob stepped up to him and for a moment just stared, his light blue eyes wolfish.

"We have a little time," he whispered.

For Ian, time just stopped. Jacob was so close and he smelled so good. But what did he mean? As Ian questioned the reality of what was happening, Jacob touched his face and brushed his fingertips across his lips. He then stepped even closer and let Ian feel how hard he was.

Ian wasn't confused any more. He leaned into Jacob and grunted at the feel of him. Slowly Jacob's hands slipped around Ian's waist to his lower back. With one hand he pulled him closer. His other hand was jammed down the back of Ian's jeans.

Ian moaned at the contact. Jacob's fingers pushed down the crack of his ass. Burying his face in the crook of his neck,

Jacob growled. The tip of his middle finger found Ian's hole and pressed in. Moaning, Ian clutched at Jacob as he fingered him. Then Jacob stopped, withdrew his hand and stepped back.

Ian stared at him, dazed and shaking.

"Strip. I want to see you," Jacob ordered him almost angrily.

More than happy to do as he was told, Ian smirked and obeyed. Rushed, they had no time for niceties. He toed off his boots. His jeans and boxers were down, off and kicked across the floor. He pulled his hoodie up over his head and threw it aside. He was standing naked in front of Jacob in one minute flat. And that was all the time Jacob gave him before he was on him again.

The urgency of knowing he was leaving made Ian crazy. With trembling fingers, he undid Jacob's fly and freed his cock. Damn, it was big and hard, and it worried him. He bit his bottom lip.

"Be right back," Jacob told him. As he walked away, he pulled his shirt off over his head and threw it aside. His jeans were slipping down his hips. Ian groaned. Fuck, he was gorgeous. His shoulders were broad. His back rippled as he moved. The muscles of his arms were hard and beautiful. Ian actually felt intimidated as he waited for him to come back. Ian was slim, had OK definition, but his body definitely didn't earn him a hunk like that.

He didn't feel any more at ease as Jacob came back. Ian's eyes traveled from his amazingly sculpted chest down to his abs and then lower. Jacob's jeans stood open with his cock sticking straight out. He was a vision.

And if that didn't scare him, the look in Jacob's eyes was deadly. He had lube and condoms in one hand and he slapped them down next to Ian on the kitchen counter. With both hands free, he grabbed Ian's face and kissed him deep and hard. Ian pushed away from him, gulping air.

"I guess that was enough kissing. Turn around," Jacob said.

He guided Ian to lean over the counter next to the sink where there was nothing for him to hit his head on. The stone countertop was cold, but Jacob's mouth trailing kisses down his back was hot. Ian gasped. Then he heard the cap from the lube bottle snap open and felt Jacob's slick fingers at his hole.

Ian groaned as Jacob's fingers pressed in without pause. He pumped them in and out as Ian slapped the counter with his hand and cried out. He was seconds from coming, but then Jacob's fingers were gone.

Ian whimpered. Looking back, Ian saw Jacob breathing hard, rolling on a condom then adding lube.

"I don't want you like that," Jacob told him. He pulled him up and made him turn around. "I want those eyes on me."

"Yes, sir," Ian said and hopped on the counter, his ass right on the edge.

Ian hooked his hands on the edge of the counter as Jacob pushed his legs up. Ian's cock was up against his abs, harder than it had ever been. He looked at Jacob as he had his head down, aiming his cock. When he raised his eyes, they were glowing with lust. He reached across Ian's body, sliding his hand up his chest. Hooking his hand on Ian's shoulder, he started to push in. Ian panted, feeling the insistent press of Jacob's cock until his body gave in to him.

Slicked up, his cock still did not slide in easily. Ian had to fight against his instinct to pull away from him. But even as it hurt, he wanted more. He wanted to be pushed over the edge of everything he ever felt. He wanted Jacob to obliterate him and be his everything.

Jacob wasn't taking his time, and Ian felt the rush of being taken hard. The bite of pain of those first few thrusts was nothing. It was smothered in the absolute bliss of having Jacob inside him. Ian had his feet up on Jacob's shoulders. His eyes were locked on Jacob's and he let out a yell every time Jacob drove into him.

With increasing speed, Jacob thrust harder and harder. Ian yelled out his name and cursed him. Folded up tight, his cock bouncing against his abs, it was pure bliss. It was a raw, bruising heaven. Ian never wanted it to stop. But it did. It ended in a burst of unbelievable pleasure and loud cries in his ears, his own and Jacob's.

His hoarse cries subsiding, Jacob slumped over him. Wide-eyed, Ian stared up at the ceiling. He held Jacob close against him, wrapped in his arms, his legs around his back.

"You gonna miss me?" Ian asked, feeling his lips brush Jacob's ear.

"Now I will," Jacob sighed into his neck.

"Damn right," Ian said, but it was killing him that Jacob was leaving.

That couldn't be the end of it. It was too good, better than any fantasy or dream. He had to be with Jacob again.

CHAPTER 8

It wasn't easy telling Toby that they would have to move. He was already making friends at his kindergarten and at Ruth's Daycare. Though Jacob tried to break the news as gently as he could, Toby didn't like hearing about their move. One of his reasons was his friend in the garden.

"We can't leave her all alone," Toby said plaintively.

"I'm sorry. We have to."

He was a good, kind boy and Jacob was proud of him for that, but it was his job to protect him. He hoped Toby would get to like Lambton as well, plus living there, they would get to see Heather more often.

Heather had a one bedroom apartment. Toby got her bedroom while Jacob took the couch. It was doubtful he would be sleeping much anyway.

It was only their second night in the apartment, another sleepless one for Jacob. After Toby was in bed, Jacob busied himself trying to figure out what to do about the house in Blystone. That would be easier if only he could think straight, but thoughts of Ian intruded.

He was too real. Every memory shot through him with painful clarity. The way Ian gritted his teeth when he entered him came back to him as sharply as the way his insides

49

gripped him. Jacob could feel his naked body and the pressure of his feet against his shoulders. He was filled with the sound of his moans and the way he yelled Jacob's name when he came.

Jacob had wanted to drink him in, never forget him. But he didn't mean to take things that far. He let himself lose control and now he was paying for it.

It was like he wanted to make his life more difficult. With everything he had on his mind, it was crazy to be obsessed with Ian. It seemed like the heart was never too busy for self-torture.

Outwardly, Jacob was calm. He had to be for Toby's sake. Leaving their new home was hard enough for both of them, but leaving Ian... Jacob couldn't dwell on that. Ian wasn't that far anyway. He might still see him. But right now Jacob wanted to be inside him, and anywhere else was too far.

Sinking into his hot, impossibly tight body obsessed him. But it was more than that. Ian didn't come back to him just as a body he had fucked. He could see his ironic, blue eyed gaze. How could that be the end when Ian's eyes told the story of their whole lives together?

Jacob stood up from the couch and paced. Going into the kitchen, he got a bottle of water. He wasn't thirsty. He just wanted to clear his mind of Ian. Toby was his number one priority and all he should be thinking about.

Toby had been in bed for hours now. Jacob was standing in the kitchen when he heard Toby's voice. He wasn't calling to him though. It sounded like he was speaking to someone. Jacob thought maybe he was just talking in his sleep. No, he hoped that he was.

Going down the hall toward the bedroom, Jacob heard his voice again and he moved faster. The bedroom door stood open. The light from the hallway cast a woman's shadow on the wall above Toby's bed.

Jacob rushed in and switched on the bedroom light. The room felt too cold. He looked around, but there was nothing there now. Sitting up in the big bed, Toby looked at him with surprise and blinked at the sudden brightness.

"Is it morning?" he asked, confused.

"No, not yet. Toby, who were you talking to?" Jacob asked though he was afraid he already knew the answer.

"The lady."

"The lady from the garden? She's here?" Sitting on the bed, Jacob looked at Toby closely. He seemed fine.

"She came to see me. She didn't want to stay there all alone," Toby said.

"You said her grandmother was there."

"She's sleeping."

Jacob kept staring around, but he didn't see or feel anything strange. The room temperature was already back to normal.

"OK. You should go back to sleep now."

Once again Jacob tucked him in, kissed the top of his head and watched him fall asleep. But this time he didn't dare leave him alone. He spent all night sitting up and watching over him.

*

Since Ian was a kid, Lorna's memorial had always been a fixture to him. He hardly glanced at it when he walked by. With everything that happened, he couldn't pass by the same way he used to. He stopped, stared at it, and wondered who had put it there.

The memorial had been there as long as he could remember, but it wasn't always standing up. It was some sort of metal stand shaped like a tripod that had shelves for holding flower pots and vases. Being a rickety, makeshift structure, it couldn't stand up to nature, not even with the spikes that held it in place. But whenever it fell over, it was always righted by some Good Samaritan.

Ian remembered that there used to be a weather-beaten plaque at the top that had Lorna's name scratched into it. It must have fallen off. Looking closer, Ian saw that only the plastic flowers were in decent shape. The flower pots had been taken over by weeds. A small bunch of wildflowers had dried in a plastic vase while other vases stood empty.

His mom used to leave flowers there. Right before she moved to Hershing, she left a white rose in a planter. The rose didn't survive though.

The wind picked up then stopped. Everything was very still. The complete silence made Ian feel as if he had gone deaf. A pot shattered suddenly and Ian jumped.

Staring at the pieces scattered in the yellow grass, he saw his breath fog up. The words "I'm so cold" were carried on a gust of wind. They sounded very close. The words might have formed in his own head.

Ian looked around. Was that her? Was that Lorna? Ian stepped closer to the memorial, but nothing else happened.

That memorial was a sad sight, but it had never been haunted before as far as he knew. He wondered if the status quo was disturbed when Jacob took Toby away. Lorna couldn't be happy about that. She might be wandering around, looking for him.

The day before, when Ian visited her grave, he hadn't noticed anything odd. Her grave was kept in a more orderly state than the memorial. The words "Beloved daughter, granddaughter and mother" were carved into white stone. Flowers weren't left to die there or vases to sit empty.

Now that he had taken a look at both places, Ian had the impression that Lorna's grave was simply a sad, quiet place.

Lorna's presence was stronger on the side of the road, where she had been killed. It was nothing like what he felt at Jacob's though. When she appeared there, her presence had a crushing weight.

Ian was tempted to go back to Jacob's house and risk an encounter with her again. He still hoped he could find out why she was there and eventually make it safe for Jacob and Toby to come back.

Lorna wasn't his only reason for wanted to go trespassing on Jacob's property. If he went back there, his reason would be Jacob, what they did, and everything they didn't get to do. Lurking around Jacob's house wouldn't bring him back though. Ian just had to breathe through the pain he felt at every thought of him.

Moving on from that tragic spot on the side of the road, Ian continued on his way into town and tried not to think about Jacob. If only they hadn't fucked, Ian wouldn't miss him this hard. He would be tormented by what might have been, but not by this throbbing ache that was taking root inside him. Now he missed Jacob in a very real, physical way. He missed every hard inch of him.

A painful, desperate need awakened inside him the first time Jacob kissed him. The need was too strong. Stirring his cock like its plaything, it ripped open his heart, left him helpless. Their fuck only intensified his feelings. That man was now Ian's obsession and the center of his world. And he was gone.

Jacob didn't say he'd call him, never promised to keep in touch. Taking his lead, Ian didn't either. He didn't know how long he'd be able to stay firm and not call up Jacob just to see how he was doing. Maybe offer to drive over.

For now, he was too proud to chase a man who didn't give him even the smallest hint that he wanted to be chased. Ian had no idea how long that would last. Already, he pictured himself falling on his knees in front of Jacob, telling him to do anything he wanted to him. Was he seeing the future or just indulging a fantasy? He didn't know. Jacob was the first guy who had ever made him feel this crazy and desperate. He felt capable of anything heroic, filthy or depraved. Mainly he felt crushed.

CHAPTER 9

As usual on the weekends, the streets of Blystone were fairly busy. It was Saturday, and Ian was on his way to do some shopping. He was in no rush. Mrs. Astor was playing cards with his dad.

Going into McMillan's Grocery, Ian grabbed a basket and walked the isles slowly. When he looked away from a shelf, he couldn't believe his eyes. Seeing him was so unexpected, Ian just gaped. There was Jacob with a shopping basket of his own. As he went up to him, Ian was dying to throw himself into his arms.

"What are you doing here?" he asked.

"Shopping. Since we are back I need to stock the fridge," Jacob said like it was no big deal.

It might not be a big deal to him, but Ian was overjoyed. To keep himself from bursting into tears or doing anything else stupid, he looked at Jacob's basket. He saw eggs, milk and bread.

"You're back," Ian said, still trying to get over the shock. He looked up at him again. Seeing Jacob's grim face, he tried not to show how happy he was.

"It's not for a good reason," Jacob told him with a sigh. "While we were gone, I found out she isn't haunting the house. She's haunting Toby."

"What do you mean?"

"She followed us to Heather's apartment. Toby saw her, and I kind of did too. I saw a shadow standing over Toby's bed. At that point I wanted to take him even further away. But I'm afraid quitting my job and moving to the other side of the country wouldn't do any good either. She told Toby that she would always be with him."

"You heard that?" Ian asked.

"No. Toby was talking to her. He told me." As Jacob shook his head and rubbed his eyes, Ian noticed how tired he looked. "I thought we could get away, but I guess it doesn't matter where we go."

"That doesn't mean you had to come here. This is where it started," Ian pointed out though this was exactly where he wanted them to be.

"Didn't see a good reason to stay away," Jacob said and looked away from Ian. That was weird. When he turned back to him, he looked kind of embarrassed. "Going away did no good, but maybe I can do some good here. I think you were on the right track. This is the place where I have the best chance of figuring this out. We're better off here anyway. She never comes inside the house. At the apartment, she was in Toby's bedroom, standing right over his bed. Unless I imagined her."

"You said Toby was talking to her," Ian said reasonably, not letting Jacob sink into denial.

"It's still hard for me to believe in something like that."

"Even after seeing her for yourself?"

"Yes. Even after that."

"Your reasons might not be good, but I'm glad you're back," Ian confessed.

"Toby is too. I dropped him off at Ruth's. He and the puppies had a happy reunion. I still want him out of the house as much as possible, so I signed him up for daycare on Saturdays too."

As they made their way to the register, Ian noticed how gloomy Jacob looked.

"Don't look so down. Remember you're not alone. I want to help you figure this out."

"Your plate is pretty full," Jacob said. "How is your dad?"

"Not great. But he's hanging in there. I was just getting him some fresh lemons for his tea," Ian said holding up a shopping basket with a half dozen of them. "Dad always gives me credit for getting him to live right. He stopped drinking and smoking when he and my mom adopted me. But I guess I was too late."

"Don't tell me you blame yourself for that?" Jacob asked him archly.

"I guess that's stupid. My dad was always terrible at taking care of himself. Now I feel like I never know how he's really doing. He's always trying to hide what he's going through."

"He's a dad," Jacob said evenly.

"Listen to you, taking his side."

"Us dads have to stick together," Jacob said with a smile.

Ian waited for Jacob to check out then they walked together toward his house. Once they were standing in front of it, they both stopped and stared. Ian could tell that Jacob was dreading going through his own front gate.

"Are you afraid to go in there?" Ian asked him.

"Not exactly. I just don't know how to fix this," he said as he stepped into his front yard and Ian followed.

"When you saw her, are you sure she didn't give you any clues about what she wanted?" Ian asked as they walked up the path to the front door.

"We didn't have a conversation," Jacob said flatly. As they went into the house, he stopped just inside. He frowned deeply. "Something I didn't tell you about. That wasn't the first time I've seen someone who was dead."

He didn't say more for a while. Then while they were in the kitchen, and Jacob was putting away groceries, he told him about it.

"Something happened to me when I was a kid. Since then, I've pretty much put it out of my mind. Until a few days ago, I wasn't sure that any of that was real. I thought maybe I was remembering something I imagined as a kid," Jacob said. "Everything that happened back then seems so unreal to me, like I dreamed it. What's happening now forced me to remember."

Jacob grabbed two beers from the fridge and handed one to Ian. They sat at the kitchen table as Jacob told him more.

"I was about the same age as Toby when I started coming across pools of water around our house. I could see water dripping and rippling, but it wasn't coming from anywhere. When I went closer, the water disappeared. Then one day, I saw a pair of bare feet standing in the water."

"That must have been terrifying," Ian said.

Jacob shook his head. "Not really. I remember I was puzzled, not afraid. After a while, I saw who the feet belonged to. It was a boy. His clothes were dirty, and he was always dripping wet. He seemed a little older than me. He just wanted to talk to me, but I had trouble making out what he was saying. I used to ask him, 'Why are you all wet? It's not raining.' I didn't really understand that this was something I wasn't supposed to see. Not until I told my parents. At first they dismissed it as just my overactive imagination. But when I kept insisting I saw him, they took me to a child psychologist. It didn't take me long to figure out that I shouldn't talk about what I saw. After a few months, there was nothing to talk about. I stopped seeing the boy. He started to fade away then he disappeared completely. After that, I never saw any kind of spirit or whatever you want to call it."

"What about that boy you saw? Did he tell you his name?

Was he someone who lived in the house?"

"I asked his name, but I'm not sure if he knew it. Toby asked Lorna her name too, but she never told him. From what I remember about that boy, he never answered any of my questions directly. Whenever I had to leave, I can remember him saying, 'Don't go.' But most of what he said didn't make much sense."

"Did you do any research on who the boy might be?"

"I didn't, but there was a well known case. A boy who used to live in our house twenty years before. He disappeared, then days later, his body was pulled from the river wrapped in a sheet. The case was never solved."

"Did he give you any clues or..." Ian asked.

"What? You want to try and solve a murder four decades old?"

"Maybe," Ian admitted.

"He only told me it was dark and that he was cold. I remember trying to give him my jacket. He told me to watch out for the bad man, but nothing specific." Jacob shook his head. "It makes me so sad now. When I was little, I didn't understand how terrible his fate was. Not that I understand much now. God, I feel so lost. How am I supposed to help Toby?" Jacob ran his hands through his hair in frustration.

"Think back," Ian told him. "You didn't have a bad experience with your ghost, right? It was the way your parents reacted that spooked you."

"True. So you're saying I shouldn't spook Toby?"

"I don't think it's necessarily a good thing for him to be talking to dead people," Ian admitted. "But he isn't upset. He doesn't seem to be in any danger."

"So far."

"This might be a problem that will solve itself. She might fade away like your little friend," Ian said optimistically. "And I'll keep digging and try to figure out why she's here."

"You think there is an answer? Like finding the killer or something?" Jacob asked.

"Or her kid. He was sent off to live with relatives, but I can't find out where. No one seems to know. There's a good chance that kid is the reason she's here, and that's why she's so focused on Toby. I'll keep digging. But you should try to communicate with her, find out what she wants."

Jacob wasn't optimistic about that idea. "My experience with her was nothing like what happened to me when I was a kid. It might be an ability I lost."

"You saw her in the garden. You saw her standing over Toby in his room."

"I saw something but mostly I felt her presence or whatever that was. And there was only a shadow at the apartment."

"I think you should try harder to see and hear her," Ian told him.

"I don't know that I want to. I still want to believe this isn't real." Jacob rubbed his eyes. Once again Ian noticed that he looked tired.

"Try anyway. We need more clues."

"And what if she's simply after Toby?" Jacob asked.

Ian dismissed the idea. "She was haunting the place before he was even born. Something else is keeping her around."

Ian got up from the table, ready to go home with his bag of lemons. As he stood up, Jacob grabbed him. His hands on Ian's shoulders, he pulled him close and kissed him. One of his hands shifted to the back of Ian's head, grabbing a handful of his hair to draw him in even closer. It was a good, hard kiss that told Ian that Jacob missed him.

When he kissed back, Ian wasn't gentle and sweet either. His kiss pushed back. It was needy and rough, trying to smother the fear of almost losing him.

Ian didn't want to let him go, but somehow Jacob still pulled away from him. "I have to go pick up Toby soon," Jacob said, out of breath.

Ian nodded, just as breathless. As they looked at each other, neither one of them wanted to move. A moment ago, Ian was ready to leave, but now it seemed so impossible. Wordlessly, he tried to tell Jacob how much he wanted him and everything else he felt.

*

Walking down the front path, Ian looked back one last time before turning onto the sidewalk. Maybe he was making sure that Jacob was still staring after him. And he was.

Jacob was only able to close the door once Ian was out of sight. It was ridiculous. He felt like he was in high school and completely at the mercy of his feelings.

Now that he had sent him away, Jacob was almost painfully hard for Ian. They had shared another hard, grappling embrace. His fault again. He wondered if they would ever share a gentle kiss. Maybe when they had more time. But there was something wild and uninhibited about Ian. Every time they touched, Jacob felt as if he was leading him down a dark path.

He had to wonder if he was just using Ian to take his mind off what was happening. Ian might be with him for the same reason. Jacob wouldn't blame him. It wouldn't do Ian any good to dwell on how sick his father was. Both Fran James and Ruth had told him that the cancer had spread too much and the chemo wasn't working. Jacob hated to think of all the pain that was going to come crashing down on Ian.

Jacob understood the need for distraction from problems one couldn't solve. At night, Jacob couldn't sleep for more than a few hours. He was restless and checked on Toby constantly. Now that he had seen that shadow over Toby's bed, he might never be able to rest easy again.

Thinking about Ian occupied the sleepless hours of the night. His stormy, dark blue eyes always seem to speak to Jacob. He felt like he needed a lifetime to take in everything that was in them. That was a frightening thought, but if he could, he would never look away from Ian's eyes.

Jacob's mind dwelled on each part of Ian in turn. His mouth came back to him – yielding to Jacob's, his tongue probing, his moans muffled but tasting so sweet in Jacob's mouth.

Outside his window, the hard wind through the branches made a clattering noise. Jacob's eyes opened to the darkness of his bedroom. The sound reminded him of what was out there and snapped him out of his fantasies.

As he watched the trees cast shifting shadows on the walls, Jacob didn't know how they could stay in this house. He didn't know where they could hide. For now, he was willing to go along with Ian's approach to the problem. Instead of running from her, he would try to figure out Lorna Hayes as if she were a puzzle.

Looking for clues, he thought back to his own childhood experience. All that taught him was that ghosts fade away either from an individual's perception or from reality. If his own experience was anything to go by, Toby might just grow out of it or choose not to see what isn't supposed to be there. Until then, Jacob had to do his best to protect him.

CHAPTER 10

*N*o matter how hard he tried to keep his expectations realistic and his feelings under control, Ian was overjoyed that Jacob was back. Sure there was still the problem of Lorna Hayes, but they would solve it, maybe even together.

Together – that made him grin, but he was getting way ahead of himself. He and Jacob had something, but what the hell was it exactly? For now, Ian wasn't going to question it. He was just going to take what he could get.

Today, that meant going over to Jacob's for Sunday lunch. The first one to greet him when he arrived at Jacob's house was Toby. He had a big smile on his face as he opened the door.

"Good to see you back," Ian told him. He was really happy to see the little guy again.

"You too! You're gonna help us eat lunch?" Toby asked.

"You need help?"

"Yeah. There's lots," Toby said making a big circle with his arms.

"Your dad must be making something good. What's for lunch?" he asked as he followed Toby into the kitchen.

Jacob was standing over a big pot simmering away on the stove. Ian looked over his shoulder. It looked and smelled good, whatever it was.

"We practically live on sandwiches," Jacob told him. "But I thought I should cook a proper meal. It's chicken and sweet potato stew."

"Smells good. Can I do anything? Set the table?" Ian offered, pointing to the table in the kitchen.

"The table is already set," Jacob told him. "We'll be eating outside. But you can grab two beers for us."

With two beers held in one hand, Ian opened the back door and they both stepped outside.

"We're really going to eat out here?" Ian asked, seeing the plates and utensils set up on the table in the garden.

"We've been eating out here since we moved in. Not as much now that the weather is colder. She hasn't bothered us," Jacob told him.

Ian was surprised that he wasn't more concerned about spending time out there. He looked around at the garden and saw nothing but foliage turning yellow and brown.

"It's a nice day for it," Ian said. The garden might be haunted but there was no sign of it on such a beautiful, sunny day. He did notice that Toby wasn't out there with them.

"Are you keeping Toby out of here?"

"I told him he could only be back here when I'm with him. So far nothing has ever happened while I was around," Jacob said.

Toby did come to join them soon after that, and the stew was really good. Ian was taking some home to his dad. After their lunch, Jacob sent Toby inside to wash his hands. Ian helped clear the table. He took their bowls into the kitchen and noticed a birthday card on the counter.

"Whose birthday is it?" he asked Jacob when they went back out.

He sat down at the table again, and he and Jacob finished their beers.

"It's my mom's. I'm sending her flowers and Toby is drawing her a card. Toby is the best son and the best grandson," Jacob said as Toby ran out to join them. He pulled him into a hug.

"I guess it's your grandma's birthday next week," Ian said.

"Yeah. I'm making her a card!" Toby said excitedly then ran inside the house again. Soon he came back out with construction paper and a box of crayons.

"I guess it's on," Ian said, seeing him ready to get to work.

Climbing into his chair, Toby painstakingly picked his first crayon, a bright green one, and looked at his dad.

"Put an H here," Jacob told him, pointing at a spot on the paper.

Toby turned to Ian and told him, "H is the ladder." He then drew two lines that came dangerously close to a V and crossed them with two other lines.

"Why don't you fill in the space between those two lines so it looks more like an H," Ian suggested.

"Is that right?" Toby asked his father.

"It's a good idea," his dad confirmed.

Just helping him write "Happy" seemed to take a million years, and the result was... creative. Seeing that both their beer bottles were empty, Ian asked, "Are we going to need more beer for the next word?"

Jacob looked like he wanted to say yes, but then he shook his head. "Better not. We'll just muscle through."

"Toby is the one doing the hard work," Ian said. He looked over at him and saw him writing much faster than he did before.

"I thought he couldn't write. Hey!" Ian said as he realized that this wasn't natural. He stood up as did Jacob.

Toby's writing had gone from a shaky, childish scrawl to jagged lines drawn firmly, but overlapped. The writing formed words that Ian couldn't quite read.

He and Jacob both held their breaths. Jacob reached out

slowly to grab Toby's hand and put a stop to it. Toby's hand kept moving, but Jacob's wouldn't.

He looked down at his hand where it had stopped in midair. Ian instinctively took hold of it. Jacob's hand felt freezing cold. Ian moved slowly toward Toby. He placed his hand over Toby's and the writing stopped. He noticed his hand was a little cold too, but not as bad as Jacob's. Jacob was rubbing his hand. He looked freaked out.

"What does it say?" Toby asked as he looked at what he had written.

Ian frowned at the writing but it overlapped too much and he still couldn't make it out.

"I'm not sure."

Jacob looked at it too. "It says 'leave' three times," he said. "Why did you write this, Toby?"

"It wasn't me. I can't write," Toby said reasonably.

"It was your hand," Jacob pointed out.

"She was holding it," Toby told him.

"She? The lady?"

Toby nodded.

"What did she want?" Ian asked.

"To write," Toby answered.

"Interrogating him is fun," Ian said, but Jacob looked extremely disturbed by this. He was keeping it under control, but only barely.

"Did she tell you anything?" Jacob asked Toby.

"No, but she was mad."

"At you?" Jacob asked and clenched his fist.

"No. She's never mad at me. She's mad at you, Ian," Toby said turning to him.

"Do you know why?" Ian asked him.

Toby shook his head.

CHAPTER 11

*Th*ey went inside and Jacob told Toby not to go outside at all, not even with him. He sent Toby to his room to draw a picture for the front of the card on a fresh piece of construction paper.

"Obviously spending time outside was a big mistake," Jacob said through gritted teeth once Toby was gone. He dropped into a chair in the kitchen and pushed his fingers through his hair.

"Keep in mind that she didn't hurt him. He wasn't even scared. And that 'leave, leave, leave' was meant for me," Ian reminded him. "She doesn't like it that I'm here. Is she jealous?"

"You think she's jealous that you're spending so much time with Toby?" Jacob asked.

"Or with you? You three make a cozy little family," Ian said.

Jacob grimaced. "Hardly."

"She might not see it that way. I did ask some more about what happened to her baby and those relatives that took him in, but I got nothing so far. No one can remember any relatives who came to either Lorna's or her grandmother's funeral. The sheriff's office doesn't know anything about them either."

"Would they give you that information?" Jacob wondered.

"Not formally, but I asked Deputy Jenkins. He's been around forever. He was clear that they had no record of any relatives." Jacob rubbed his hand.

"Is it still cold?" Ian asked. He took Jacob's hand in his own and started entwining their fingers together.

"No. It's OK. But keep doing that." He was giving Ian a mischievous look one minute then he grew thoughtful again. "Is it going to do any good to keep Toby out of the back garden? She visited him at Heather's. She could follow him anywhere."

"Maybe she can't appear just anywhere?" Ian said, trying to sound hopeful. "Toby hasn't seen her anywhere else until you went to your sister's apartment."

Jacob leaned forward with his head in his hands. "God, how am I supposed to protect him from something like this?"

Ian leaned forward too and put his hand on Jacob's biceps. "Remember she's not hostile to Toby or you, just to me. This won't last forever. We'll figure it out."

Jacob raised his head. "Thank you. I find the groping very reassuring."

Ian pulled his hand back. "I wasn't groping." Ian leaned back indignantly while Jacob gave him a sly smile. "You don't even know groping. If I groped you, you wouldn't be sitting there smirking. You'd be tackling me to the floor and ripping my pants off."

"Maybe some other time," Jacob said still looking smug.

"I'll consider that an open invitation to jump you," Ian warned him. Then the uncertain look on Jacob's face made him whisper, "It's easy to get rid of me. Just tell me you don't feel what I feel."

Jacob looked into his eyes then shook his head. "I'm not going to lie just to get rid of you."

Ian stared at him, wondering if he heard him right. Did he know what Ian felt? He couldn't. The feeling was too strong and too crazy. Jacob would run if he knew how bad Ian had it for him.

Jacob got more serious again. "I better go see what Toby is up to," he said and got up.

Ian got up too. "And I better go relieve Mrs. Astor."

As they both stood right where they had last kissed, Ian looked into Jacob's eyes a little too long and then he couldn't look away. Hell, he didn't even want to breathe. Just like last time, it was as if time had stopped, and something had to happen for it to start up again.

In slow motion, Jacob leaned in and gave him a quick, soft kiss on the lips. Ian's eyes fell closed. He leaned into it, but Jacob pulled away.

"Tease," Ian whispered.

He opened his eyes to see Jacob standing a little back from him. It might have been what he considered a safe distance. The smirk was gone from his face. His eyes had an intense gleam before he turned away to call Toby to come and say bye to Ian.

The whole way as he walked home, Ian felt off balance. It was as if that soft kiss had permanently shifted his center of gravity. He had other reasons to feel unsettled. That thing with Lorna telling him to leave didn't sit well with him. He sure as hell wasn't going to give up on Jacob or Toby because of a ghost.

As he arrived home, he wondered what his dad would think about all this especially about Ian seeing a dead woman. But he didn't want to talk to him about death. Death had nothing to do with his dad. That's what he had to believe.

A few hours later, Ian was setting the table for dinner when he noticed his dad looking at him.

"What?" Ian asked.

"You look more cheerful," his dad said.

"Do I?" Ian said evasively and looked away.

"Any particular reason?"

"Are you fishing?" Ian accused him.

"Who? Me?" His dad smiled. "I'm just noticing. Being observant. It's a good look on you. I'm glad I got to see it."

"See what?"

"My Ian in love."

Ian gaped at him. "Hey, don't make pronouncements about me."

"Am I wrong?" his dad asked, but he knew he was right.

"I don't know. It's too soon for that," Ian said defensively.

"It's not too soon if it's what you feel."

"Feelings are dangerous," Ian said in a gloomy voice.

His dad laughed at him. "You must have it bad."

"Stop being right, Dad."

He was glad his dad was enjoying seeing him going crazy over Jacob. To Ian, there was too much uncertainty and tension in what was happening between him and Jacob. He wanted Jacob to feel the same thing he did, but he couldn't read him. Sometimes there was a look in his eyes that seemed to be warning him off.

Of course, he had a lot on his mind. Ian wasn't about to pressure him. Jacob wasn't just an object of his lust. But until he could nail him down, or just nail him again, he would wait, dream about him and jerk off to every remembered inch of him.

CHAPTER 12

*S*ince his dad was so interested in his love life, Ian wanted him to meet Jacob – just casually, as someone who recently moved into town, no big deal. He stopped by their place one evening after dinner and invited Jacob and Toby to come by for a quick visit. It turned out that Jacob had an overseas conference call scheduled for work and couldn't come.

Hearing the invitation, Toby offered his services. "I want to see your dad. You know my dad. I don't know your dad. That's not fair," he said.

"I want to tell you, my dad is very sick," Ian said to him.

"Oh, no. Does he have the flu? A flu is really bad. Dad had it. It was terrible." Toby looked at his dad with disapproval for getting sick.

"It's not the flu, but it's pretty bad. My dad can't do very much. You still want to see him?" Ian asked.

Toby nodded, not discouraged at all. "Can I go?" he asked his dad.

"Sure you can," he said and gave him a hug. "Be good for Ian. Remember you're my big guy."

"No, you're my big guy," Toby said to him.

"Yes, I am," Jacob admitted and Toby giggled.

"Big guy," Toby said giving his dad a big grin.

The two of them set off with Toby taking Ian's hand as soon as they stepped out the door. It was already getting dark. The sky had turned dark blue with a glowing orange line along the horizon. Peering around him curiously, Toby seemed excited but a little bit scared too as they walked out past the edge of town. Ian held his hand tighter to reassure him.

To distract him, he told him stories from his childhood. As they passed Lorna's memorial, Ian told him how he was trying to catch a frog from the stream, and it jumped on his head. Toby giggled so hard, he couldn't ask Ian about what the funny contraption was. Ian wasn't sure what he would have told him if he did. After all, Jacob hadn't told him Lorna was dead. Ian sure as hell wasn't going to do it.

When they arrived at the house, Ian announced them from the door, "Hey, Dad. A friend of mine wanted to meet you!"

Toby grinned at being called his friend.

"Wipe you feet," Ian told him. His sneakers had gotten a little dirty from walking by the side of the road.

Going into the kitchen, they found his dad sitting in his window seat.

Toby ran right up to him and took a close look. "Ian said you're sick. When you're sick, you have to eat soup," Toby informed him.

"I like soup," Ian's dad said.

"You have to put fish crackers in it. Then it's good."

Dad agreed. "Of course. So they can swim."

"Yes!" Toby said.

"I haven't even introduced you guys, and you're already yakking it up," Ian said. "This is Toby. He's my friend and so is his dad, Jacob."

"We're all friends," Toby said. "And I know who you are. You're Ian's dad."

"Yes, I am. Nice to meet you."

"Nice to meet you too!" Toby shouted then a sight out the

window caught his eye.

Ian and his dad turned to look too. Three horses were out there in the meadow, two gray, one white. On a moonlit evening, they practically glowed. Toby was very excited to see them.

"They belong to the Suttons. They bring them to the field to graze," Dad told him. "Ian can take you out there for a closer look."

"But not too close," Ian said. He could picture Toby wanting to go right up to them and pet them.

He grabbed a flashlight and gave one to Toby too. Ian warned him to watch where he stepped. Once they were out behind the house, Toby pointed his flashlight everywhere but at the ground.

With Ian lighting their way, they walked over the field toward the fence. The horses were on the other side, grazing a little. Seeing them, Toby got excited and wanted to climb the fence.

"Horses kick," Ian told him. "And they bite."

Ian was relieved that the horses weren't feeling friendly. They didn't come up to them even when Toby called them over.

"They aren't coming," he complained to Ian. "Maybe we have to call their names. Do you know their names?"

"Sorry, I don't. We'll just watch them from here."

They did that for a while. Every time one of the horses turned, Toby waved and said "Hi!" to them.

When one of the horses neighed and shook his mane, Toby said, "He's saying hi back."

Ian had quite a time getting him to leave.

"You'll get us in trouble with your dad," he told Toby.

Actually he had already texted Jacob with updates, especially about Toby's enthusiasm for horses. "You'll have to get him one of his own," he had told him.

73

"OK. The horses are getting sleepy. We better go," Ian said when he decided time was up.

"Aww," Toby complained. He would have stayed out there all night.

Going up to the back door, Ian opened it and heard a familiar, deep voice say, "It's a pleasure to meet you, sir."

Then Ian heard his dad say, "Just call me Larry. So you're the reason my son's eyes are glowing."

Ian rushed into the kitchen to keep his dad from embarrassing him even more. He saw Jacob standing there, grinning at him.

Toby went up to him, and pulled on his arm. "You have to come see the horses. They are sleepy so you have to hurry."

"Aren't you sleepy?" Jacob asked him. "It's almost your bedtime."

"Already?" Toby said with a pout.

"Yes."

Jacob and Toby said goodbye to his dad.

"Eat lots of soup and get better soon," Toby told Ian's dad as they were leaving.

His dad gave him a smile, but the look in his eye told Ian that he knew how unlikely that was. Ian had to work hard to believe that his father might recover. He had to ignore how thin and frail his dad was. He had to look past all the pill bottles and the oxygen tank that helped him breathe more and more often.

From the porch, he stared after Jacob and Toby as they were walking to Jacob's car. Ian wanted to believe that that was him and his dad. He was a little kid and his dad was big and strong. His dad would protect him and nothing could hurt him because his dad was invincible.

CHAPTER 13

*N*ext Saturday, when he knew Toby was in daycare, Ian went over to Jacob's. He didn't pretend his reason was innocent. As soon as Jacob opened the door, Ian was on him.

"I know you're worried about the ghost. I don't have any new information. I'm here on a humanitarian mission – to help you unwind," Ian said as he pressed himself against Jacob and kicked the front door closed behind him.

"You're so selfless," Jacob mocked him while acting aloof.

"Give it to me on a more regular basis and I won't have to find excuses to get what I want," Ian said. He pushed Jacob up against the wall.

Jacob's attitude didn't change even as Ian was grinding into him. He was still acting superior. That only made Ian more hot and impatient. He shoved Jacob into the living room and pushed him to sit on the couch. Taking off his jacket, Ian sat next to him. Then he draped his arm over Jacob's lap and let his hand rest between his knees.

"Just getting comfortable," Ian said as he leaned into his shoulder.

While Ian wore an innocent expression on his face, his hand slid up between Jacob's legs. Ian squeezed his cock and felt it get even harder. Its outline was growing so clear. He had to free it. He had to have it right now.

As Ian breathed hard, he unzipped him. Handling his cock properly for the first time, Ian looked hard at Jacob. His eyes were heavy lidded with the desire, his jaw clenched like he wanted to fight against what was happening. He better not.

He swallowed hard as he wondered what Jacob would taste like. His cock was hard and heavy in Ian's hand and he was dying to bring it to his mouth. Ian couldn't believe they fucked and he never got a taste of him.

Ian rushed to kneel between his legs. As Jacob shifted his hips down, Ian parted and licked his lips. His fingers wrapped around the shaft and he bowed his head over Jacob's cock. His mouth watering, he licked the head getting his first salty, good taste of Jacob.

He had to tell himself to breathe. He hadn't been this nervous giving head since his first time. As he took the head of Jacob's cock in his mouth, Ian's eyes fell closed. He sucked and moaned contentedly around his cock as he let it further into his mouth. This felt too good.

Ian's focus was on Jacob's cock and nothing else. Every vein as it passed over his tongue made him shudder and get harder. That reminded him that his own cock needed attention.

He fumbled with his own fly and freed his cock. He gave it a few absentminded strokes as Jacob reached out for Ian and played with his hair. He brushed it back from his face, and Ian let a long moan travel up his cock. Jacob threw his head back and arched up off the couch a little. Ian didn't let Jacob rush him. With his eyes closed, Ian savored him and sucked as slow as he could to make it last.

Liking the control, Ian built up speed eventually. Now Jacob was getting ready to come, and the look in his eyes was almost savage with impatience. Ian loved it. He sucked harder and faster, desperate to see him come and drink him in.

With a grunt, Jacob's hips came up and Ian had to struggle to keep up as he came. Ian came too, lost in a flood of Jacob's come, his name said in a harsh growl as Jacob gripped his hair with one hand and raked his back with the other.

"Fuck, Ian," he said as he slumped back.

He seemed less like an animal now and more like a guy who just had the life sucked out of him. Ian grinned at the picture of a job well done.

"Proud of yourself," Jacob asked him, a sharp look coming back to his eyes.

"You bet," Ian said as he got up and climbed on his lap. Straddling him, he leaned down and kissed him.

After some thorough kissing, they made themselves decent and went to the kitchen. Ian took a seat at the table, and Jacob made him a sandwich.

"You're not having anything?"

"Not hungry," Jacob said as he set the plate with Ian's sandwich in front of him. He then took a seat across from him at the kitchen table.

"You can't let stress get to you. You have to eat," Ian lectured him. Getting up, he grabbed a knife. He cut his sandwich and gave half of it to Jacob.

Jacob bit into it grudgingly. "I need to eat. I need to sleep, but I can't do much of either."

"You can't sleep?"

"I was never a good sleeper."

"I thought I did a good job back there," Ian said pointing back toward the living room. "But you only look a little more relaxed. Should I have another go at you?"

"Feel free, but I'll be tense again in seconds. How can this be happening? A dead woman is haunting my son. This shouldn't be real."

"You want me to explain ghosts?" Ian asked, not that he could.

"You could tell me that this all makes sense somehow."

"It doesn't. This is crazy, but it's happening," Ian told him bluntly.

"I just want it to stop. I want my boy to be safe."

"She hasn't done anything to hurt him or even frighten him," Ian reminded him. Instead of sensing an ominous, bone chilling presence, Toby saw something luminous and friendly that tugged at his heart. "Since you're a hopeless case, I'm going to go, look in on my dad," Ian said as he got up.

When he was a few steps from the front door, Ian turned around.

"I'm going to leave through the back," he told Jacob. "I want to see if your ghost has anything to say to me."

"And I thought you were here for me. Should I be jealous?" Jacob asked.

"I don't mind if you get jealous, but not of a ghost. I want you to get crazy jealous of an awesome, hunky guy who has the hots for me."

"Is there a guy?" Jacob asked, his expression turning dark.

"Just you," Ian said and grinned. He hoped Jacob got his message. He wasn't sure though. Jacob frowned at his words.

"What's the problem?" Ian asked him. "I'm ready to get serious. Why do I get the impression that you don't like the idea?" He had noticed that look in Jacob's eyes before, but he didn't want to push him. Right now, he was in the mood to push both the ghost and Jacob.

"Do you even know what you're taking on?" Jacob asked him.

"The best kid in the world. And you too," Ian told him. He was nervous as soon as he said the words. What if Jacob shut him down?

Jacob looked taken aback. "I don't think you know what you're saying," he said sounding more than a little scared.

"What has you so worried about me?" Ian asked, not that he wanted to hear it.

"No matter how much I want you, when I look at you, I see a young guy who isn't ready for my kind of total commitment," Jacob stated.

"That's because you aren't looking hard enough," Ian told him, getting kind of mad.

Jacob narrowed his eyes at him. "I'm looking pretty hard."

"And you don't think I'm right for you?"

"I don't think you're ready. I decided to have Toby because I was ready to be a dad. I was done waiting for a man to come into my life who wanted the same thing I did."

"Well, you can stop waiting. I'm here now."

Jacob couldn't help laughing. He tried to get all serious again, but a smile just wouldn't leave his face as he looked at Ian.

"That's a good start," Ian told him as he smiled back. "You make peace with the reality of me in your life, and I'll go out and talk to your ghost." Ian pointed his thumb out the back door and turned to go.

"Should I come out there with you?" Jacob offered.

Ian turned back and gave him a quick kiss. "What a good boyfriend you are. But I think I better try by myself."

Ian didn't wait for Jacob to get over being called his boyfriend, he just stepped outside. It looked peaceful out there, bright with sunshine but cold from the wind that was blowing the leaves around. Ian walked to the back the garden slowly, almost like he was trying to sneak up on any ghostly presence that might be lurking there.

A few steps from the bench, it hit him. The noise of the wind became deafening, but the air grew still and freezing cold. Shivering uncontrollably, Ian had trouble breathing. He forced himself to take a lungful of cold air and he spoke.

"Can you hear me? Why did you want me to leave?" he asked.

His eyes darted around. Not being able to see her, he didn't know where to look.

"Why do you hate me?" he asked. It was crazy to expect an answer, but he had to ask.

Amid all the noise, a rasping sound was rising and falling. She might have been trying to speak. Ian listened closely and tried to decipher it.

Then he heard, "Ask your father."

It was like the rushing of the wind was doing a bad imitation of speech through dry leaves and rusty windpipes. But he was sure that he made out those words. What the hell was that supposed to mean?

CHAPTER 14

After telling Jacob what he thought he heard, Ian went home confused. Was he really supposed to ask his dad about the ghost of Lorna Hayes? His dad did grow up here, but what could he know about her? From what Ian remembered, his mom and dad were in North Caroline when Lorna died. That's where they adopted him.

Even if it seemed unlikely, Ian was going to ask his dad anyway. He might end up sounding like an idiot, but it was important for Toby's sake that they find out whatever they could about Lorna.

First Ian made sure that his dad was well enough to talk. He seemed to be doing OK so Ian pulled a chair from the breakfast table a little closer to the window seat. Then he dived right in.

"Dad, do you know anything about Jacob's house, number 211? It's where Lorna Hayes used to live. Or about her family or anything at all?" Ian rambled. He wasn't sure what to ask.

At his words, his father's expression darkened. "Why would..." he stammered then coughed.

"Dad? You OK?" Ian asked and went over to rub his back. He handed him his water bottle.

"Why did you ask me that?" his dad wanted to know once he

was able to speak.

Ian didn't want to tell him about the apparition. "Something I heard."

"How would you hear? Did your mother tell you something?" his dad asked. He was so agitated.

"Dad, what would she tell me?" Ian asked, confused.

"Nothing. There's nothing to tell." His father seemed so pale now.

Ian didn't want to upset him. It sounded like his mom might know something, so he asked, "Dad, should I call Mom about this?"

"No. Don't." His father was vehement.

"Then you better tell me about it. What's going on? But don't get worked up. Take it easy," Ian told him.

His father slumped over. "Your mother lived there."

"What? Where?" Ian said, not understanding him. "At 211. I thought Mom moved here when you two got married."

His father shook his head. He looked so tired as he spoke. "No. Not Beth. Your birthmother."

For a while Ian just stared. His brain couldn't put this together. What his father said sounded like his mother... "Wait. What? Are you telling me..."

"Your mother was Lorna Hayes," his father said in a low voice.

For a while Ian just sat there stunned. He stared into space then at his dad, but his dad refused to meet his eyes.

"Why am I only hearing this now?" Ian asked. He was trying to put this together in his head, but nothing made sense. His brain still couldn't accept what his father said.

"There were circumstances. I... It seemed better not to tell you."

"Oh, my God. I'm the baby she had by the side of the road! How could you not tell me that?" Ian was shaking now as it all started to hit him.

"I'm sorry."

"You said I was abandoned in front of a fire station in North Carolina," Ian said. That was the story his parents had told him.

"It was too hard to tell you the truth," his dad said, his voice barely above a whisper.

"You lied."

"Yes. I'm sorry, Ian. When you were little, we didn't want you to know something like that. Later on, it got harder to tell you. We..."

Ian cut him off. "I walk by her memorial every time I go into town. The place where she died, where I was born. How could you keep that from me?"

"I'm sorry." His father hung his head.

"Could you tell me something other than 'sorry'? How did this happen?" Ian demanded.

"Beth and I had been married for ten years and we had no children. We decided maybe that's how it was supposed to be. With my drinking problem, it seemed just as well. Then you were there, you needed parents. Your great-grandmother was your only relative. When her health was failing and she couldn't take care of you any more, we went to her and offered to adopt you."

"And my biological father?" Ian asked.

"We went to him. He was willing to give up his parental rights."

"Willing or eager?" Ian said, remembering what Mr. Vinik had told him.

His dad didn't answer him, but Ian already knew the story.

"Why did it have to be a secret?"

"Your mother and I thought it was best. With what happened to Lorna, you would have been living under a cloud. After your great-grandmother died, you were taken away by the lawyer who handled the adoption. We got you from him, but we didn't want to bring you back here. We moved away for a while. I took a teaching position in North Carolina. When we came back to town, you were two years old. No one made a connection between you and Lorna's baby. We said we adopted you while we were living in North Carolina."

"I kind of get why you lied to everyone else, but why did you have to lie to me?" Ian asked. This was too big a secret to keep from him.

"It was too hard..."

"Stop," Ian said through gritted teeth. "Hard or not, you should have told me."

Ian looked at his dad and saw that he didn't look too good.

"I think you should lie down." Ian stood up and went over to take his arm. He helped him up and to his bed. With his dad moving so slowly, it took a while. Though he was out of breath, his dad murmured "I'm sorry" several times.

Ian stayed to watch over his father until he fell into a restless sleep. Tiptoeing out of his father's bedroom, Ian paced the house, trying to absorb what he had learned today.

He thought about calling his mother then decided he needed to talk to her in person. For now, there was no one he could talk to. All he could do was wait for his father to wake up so he could give him some dinner.

It turned out that his father couldn't eat much, but he did manage to keep down the little he ate. After dinner, he sat by the window and watched the nighttime landscape outside.

That's when Ian decided to go and see Jacob. He had to. After everything he found out, Ian needed to talk to Jacob right now.

He couldn't believe how much he needed to see him. He practically ran to his house. Once he got there, out of breath, he knocked softly. He didn't want to wake up Toby, who was probably in bed by now.

Jacob opened the door. Surprised to see him, he said Ian's name like a question. At first Ian didn't say anything. He was busy holding himself back. All he wanted to do was rush into Jacob's arms.

From the look on his face, Jacob could tell something was wrong. He frowned at Ian worriedly.

"Get in here," Jacob told him.

When Ian didn't move, he pulled him in by his arm.

"Sorry, I know it's late," Ian said as Jacob led him to the couch in the living room and made him sit down.

Jacob sat down next to him and turned to face him. "It's fine. What's going on?"

"I..." Ian stammered. He couldn't even say it. Then he felt Jacob take his hand. Ian fought to get the words out through gritted teeth. "I talked to my dad about Lorna Hayes. I can't even... I found out something crazy. She's my mother. And I'm the baby she gave birth to just before she died."

Jacob was silent for a moment. Then he squeezed Ian's hand. "How is that possible?"

"Lorna's grandmother let my parents adopt me. They hid the truth from everyone, especially me." Ian's mind reeled every time he thought about it.

Jacob was still holding his hand. He grabbed it tighter and pulled Ian against him. Grunting softly with surprise, Ian settled against his chest, his face in the crook of his neck. Feeling the stubble of Jacob's chin rub against his temple, Ian moaned his name.

Now that Jacob's arms were around him, Ian practically climbed into his lap. He nestled against him, pushing at him, wanting to bury himself and hide from the turmoil inside him. He felt Jacob wrap his arms around him tighter.

Damn, it felt good to be held like that – long and hard like Jacob would never let go. Ian could just live in that tight embrace forever.

"What are you going to do now?" Jacob asked, rubbing his fingertips through Ian's hair.

"I'm going home for now," Ian said straightening. "I want to check on my dad. He's pretty upset. Tomorrow I'm going to go see my mom. She lied to me too. I want to hear what she has to say."

As he walked him to the door, Jacob still held his hand. "I think your father did a good thing when he adopted you."

"I'll try and remember that."

Jacob stopped Ian before he could step through the front door. He cupped the back of Ian's head to bring him in closer and kissed him. Ian's heart was pounding so hard and loud as their mouths met and the kiss deepened. Their lips sealed together. Jacob's tongue thrust into his mouth.

He could kiss him forever, but Toby was just down the hall. They couldn't risk him catching them trying to devour each other. Ian slowly pulled back until their lips were only touching, and they were leaning on each other, breathing hard.

"I told you you were a good boyfriend," Ian whispered in Jacob's ear and kissed him on the cheek. He straightened and walked out the door.

"I'm here if you need me," Jacob called out after him, proving his point.

CHAPTER 15

*Th*e next day, Ian wanted to see his mom, but he found out that she was spending the weekend with some friends. On Monday, he couldn't talk to her until she came back from work. That left him with time to kill before he could drive to see her.

He decided to use the time to fill in some gaps in his knowledge about Lorna Hayes. When Ian tried to talk to him again, his dad got upset and told him to leave it alone. Ian backed off and tried other sources. He poked around in the archives at the town library and did some research online.

Lorna's story was something he heard about all his life, but he never paid much attention to it. Now he knew it was his story, and he wanted to know it inside and out. His dad might want to keep him in the dark, but other people in town didn't know he was Lorna Hayes' son. They would talk.

Ian went looking for Mr. Vinik. He considered asking someone else this time, but he already gave him an excuse for wanting to know about Lorna. Ian didn't want to start from scratch with someone else. He wasn't in the mood for telling more lies.

At the same time, he wasn't ready to go around town and tell everyone that Lorna Hayes was his mother. His own reluctance did give him a taste of why his parents had kept this from him, but not why they kept the secret for this long.

He met up with Mr. Vinik at Carlton's again and bought him a beer. Ian still couldn't legally order a beer for himself, though he really wanted one. He sat there with coffee and asked Mr. Vinik to flesh things out a little more for him.

"I wanted to know more about what happened to Lorna Hayes. Can you tell me about her boyfriend?" Ian had read what there was in old newspaper articles, but that wasn't much.

"Don't you go writing about him," Mr. Vinik warned him. "His people have money. And his wife's people have even more money. They'll drag you into court so fast..."

"I won't. I'm just curious," Ian assured him, but his attitude did explain why he found so little about him in the old articles. "Was he definitely the child's father or was that just a rumor?" That piece of information was really important to Ian.

Mr. Vinik confirmed it. "The police made him take a DNA test, and sure enough, that baby was his. He wanted nothing to do with that kid though. None of his people did. They just wanted to wash their hands of the whole thing, throw out the baby with the bathwater, you could say. Lorna's grandmother was more than happy to have him. She was a sweet lady."

"What was his name?" Ian asked. He almost expected to hear his own name in answer.

"She called the baby Luke."

Ian nodded and took a sip of his coffee to cover his reaction. That had once been his name, not Ian.

"And the father's name was Kurt Dufresne, right?"

"Dufresne is right. That name right there explains a lot. Not one of the Dufresnes was any good," Mr. Vinik said, shaking his finger at Ian. "They were all money-grubbing bastards from way back. Kurt's father was a state senator, you might have heard of him, Randy Dufresne. One scandal after another."

Ian nodded, but the first time he came across his name was in the articles about Lorna's unsolved murder.

"He served a few months for embezzling from some charity. That and being a state senator are his two claims to fame. His son only did one thing. He married the only daughter of Harry Litchfield. You know who he is, I bet."

"Everyone does."

"Darn right. Dufresnes were rich once, not as much lately. But the Litchfields, they are filthy, stinking, disgusting rich, rich enough to make you puke." Mr. Vinik slapped the table. Then he took a swig of his beer and continued. "Kurt's family didn't want some illegitimate kid messing up his chances to marry into that kind of money. Still can't believe that Litchfield girl would want him after what happened to poor Lorna. But, hey, who can figure out the female mind. Sure as hell not me."

After that Ian got a few more pieces of information. It all added up to Kurt Dufresne as the most likely killer. The thought of it made Ian sick. He hated the idea that this man lived in luxury after having killed his birthmother.

Kurt now lived in Mapleview. That wasn't good news for Ian if he wanted to confront the man. Mapleview was an exclusive community with security at every gate. Ian was determined to go there, but he didn't know how he would get in.

Even as he drove to see his mom Monday afternoon, Ian tried to think of a way to get into Mapleview. By the time he parked in front of his mom's brownstone in Hershing, he hadn't come up with anything. She wasn't back from work yet, so he just sat on the steps and waited.

When she arrived, his mom got out of the car with a worried look. She took slow, careful steps toward him.

"Your dad?"

Ian got up. "He's the same. I just wanted to talk to you," he said, seeing now what she was thinking.

His mom slumped over a little and put her hand on her chest with relief.

"Sorry. I didn't mean to scare you," Ian told her as they went up the steps to her place.

The second they were inside, his mom put a hand on his shoulder and took off her heels. All his life Ian had been telling her, "Just wear normal shoes."

"These legs were made for high heels. Just look at them," she would tell him.

At that point, Ian did everything but check out his mom's legs. "Mom, stop being proud of your legs. It's weird."

"They're my best feature. Ask your dad," she had said when they were still married.

That's when Ian would groan.

Then his dad would say, "Don't worry, son. I love your mother for her brilliant mind."

Ian stood in the hallway of his mom's place, amazed at how happy they all were once. Was that real?

"What's wrong?" his mom asked him. Both her hands were on his shoulders now.

Ian met her concerned gaze and answered her with one name. "Lorna Hayes."

His mom flinched away from him.

"Is it so bad that I know?" Ian asked her, seeing her reaction.

She looked at him strangely for a moment, and Ian wondered if there was something about this that he didn't understand. Then his mom shook her head. "No. Your father told you?"

"He did, but only because I heard something that made me ask him about Lorna. How could you keep this from me?"

His mom looked regretful. "Let's go sit," she told him. "My

feet are killing me."

Ian almost told her that thing about wearing normal shoes. Without saying anything, he followed her to the living room decorated in cream and light blue and a few distressed things here and there.

His mom sat down on the sofa with a sigh. Ian took a seat next to her.

"It's not easy to shake up someone's whole world, especially when it's your own child. You're asking me why we didn't find it easy to take away your peace of mind?"

"But once I was old enough..." Ian said.

"You were still my baby. Just like you're my baby now," his mom said with tears in her eyes.

Ian looked down. He wanted to be mad at her, but she made that really hard. All his life his mom had been like that – tickling him when he was about to throw a tantrum, drawing funny pictures for him when he was grouchy. Now she took his hand.

"We should have told you. We put it off too long," she told him and squeezed his hand. "This is the worst possible time for you to find out. I'm sorry."

"I know I have to take it easy on Dad," he assured her.

"You want something to eat?" she asked him.

"No. I want to go back to Dad. Sorry I surprised you," Ian said and got up.

"If you want to rant and rave, vent at someone, I'm here. OK?"

Ian hugged her instead. "I love you, Mom," he said and left.

The next evening, Ian found time to go see Jacob. It was after dinner. Toby was busy with kindergarten homework, and Ian was sitting with Jacob in the living room. The TV was on mute, its light flickering over them.

Ian had already kept Jacob updated. He texted him the broad

strokes, now he was filling in the blanks.

"I know it's crazy to think that I can figure out who killed her after all this time," Ian said, shaking his head. "One of the things I found out was the reason Lorna was out there so late. It was ten at night when she died. Her grandmother told the police they had a fight. Lorna went for a walk. She liked to go up to the bridge, the one I showed you. By the time she was killed she must have been on her way back into town. She was eight months pregnant. That probably slowed her down."

"How did the killer find her on a road at night?" Jacob asked.

"It's the main road into town. If Kurt or someone from his family was coming to see her, they might have just spotted her on the side of the road."

"So it was a crime of opportunity? The killer just got lucky?" Jacob sounded skeptical, but it was the only explanation Ian could think of.

"I looked up what I could about the case online. There was some publicity about it, but not too much about Kurt being involved. I think the local papers were afraid of his family. From what I could find, he had a flimsy alibi. Two of his friends claimed he was hanging with them at the time, but they might have easily lied for him. The police could never place him anywhere near Blystone though. Other than proving he was my father, they didn't have a case against him." Ian shuddered thinking of it again. How could he do it? Maybe it wasn't him. Kurt's father maybe?

Seeing how upset he was, Jacob rubbed his back. "With all of that, I can understand not wanting to tell a little kid about what happened to Lorna and who might have killed her." Jacob sounded a little too reasonable for Ian's liking. Noticing the dirty look he was giving him, Jacob said, "Sorry. I'm just putting myself in your parents' shoes."

"But later on, when I was old enough to be able to handle it, they should have told me."

Jacob shook his head. "I wouldn't be able to tell a child the story of his birth if it was like yours no matter how old he was. I don't hear you announcing the news to all of Blystone," Jacob pointed out.

Ian only grumbled. Then he told Jacob what else he had been up to. "I did some research on where Kurt is now. He's living it up. I don't know what kinds of answers I can expect from him, but I'm going to go see him. Any ideas on how I can get into Mapleview?"

"Mapleview." Jacob whistled. "I don't like your chances. Maybe try approaching him somewhere else."

Ian had been looking into that as well. "A bunch of companies have Kurt Dufresne listed as a board member. A board meeting is scheduled for next week at this commercial real-estate firm. If I stake out the place, I might catch Dufresne coming out from the meeting. But I didn't want to wait till next week."

"It's a better option than trying to get past security at Mapleview. Unless you think having security tell Dufresne his son is at the gate, will get you in?"

"I'm pretty sure that would keep me out, not get me in. I guess I'll have to wait till next week. Damn."

"Did you say a bad word," Toby asked. He had sneaked up on them. He was standing there holding a drawing.

"Want to show me your drawing?" Ian asked to sidestep the issue of the bad word.

Toby looked very excited about it. He ran over to Ian and showed him... something. Or three things? Thank God he identified them before Ian had to ask. "It's the horses!"

"Oh. Very nice. And those are stars." Ian pointed to the very big stars surrounded by dark blue lines. "I'm taking a picture of it. I'm going to show my dad." While Jacob admired the drawing, Ian got out his phone.

"You think your dad will like it?" Toby asked.

"Sure he will," Ian said as he snapped a few pictures of it.

"Give it to him," Toby said and offered Ian the drawing.

"Thank you," Ian said and gave him a hug.

Toby looked very happy. Ian decided to take some pictures of him holding the drawing. Toby smiled, held the drawing in one hand and waved with the other.

CHAPTER 16

*T*oby's drawing of yellow horses against a dark blue sky full of big stars was propped up on the edge of Dad's window seat. He was delighted when Ian gave it to him.

"You used to make me terrible drawings too. Not to mention all those arts and crafts projects. There's nothing more beautiful than something made by a child's hand," his dad said with tears in his eyes.

He was resting now, and Ian was doing the dinner dishes. Ian was in a constant state of tension waiting for next week's board meeting. He wanted to talk to Kurt Dufresne now, but there was no way to do that.

Good thing he could count on Jacob to distract him. He called Ian often, and just hearing his voice pushed everything else out of his head. Tonight's phone call was even better than the others.

"Toby is sleeping over at Fran's tonight. She just picked him up. Do you think you might want to stop by?" Jacob asked.

"I'll be right over. That best boyfriend medal is so gonna be yours."

Ian rushed over there, taking the car for once. He didn't want to miss a minute of time he could be spending with Jacob. As soon as Jacob opened the front door, Ian threw himself into his arms, and not gently either. Jacob grunted and then kissed him.

"I guess I better help you get rid of some of this stress before you break my bones," Jacob said.

"Wanting to help me out like that, you are so generous."

Jacob only smirked wickedly. Who would think a mild-mannered dad could ever get such a predatory look in his eyes? He kissed Ian again and dragged him to his bedroom.

His first time in there and Ian hardly got a chance to look around. All he saw were dark colors, traditional furnishings. Oh, hell, he didn't care, especially when Jacob was holding him close and kissing his neck and groping him everywhere.

Ian reached under Jacob's shirt, needing to feel him. Jacob was brushing his lips over Ian's earlobe then kissing the side of his face. As he turned his head and his mouth found Jacob's, Ian unzipped his fly.

Jacob did the same to him. He tugged down Ian's jeans roughly until he freed his cock. He grasped it and squeezed it just once before taking Ian's jeans all the way down. Ian had to grab his shoulders for support so he wouldn't fall over. Then he got out of his sweatshirt.

Jacob's hand was back on his cock but light as a feather. "That feels nice," Jacob growled in his ear. His fingers loose, he was pumping his cock too lightly.

The torturous, gentle slide of his fingers made Ian clutch at him and thrust into his hand, but he just couldn't get enough friction.

"Oh, fuck you," Ian said to him as he jammed his hand down the front of Jacob's pants. He wasn't gentle at all.

Jacob groaned. "You're so sweet. What should I do with this dirty mouth?" Jacob kissed his lower lip, and Ian dropped to his knees in front of him.

Jacob's balls went into his mouth one then the other. Then his cock was sliding over Ian's tongue, crowding his throat.

Jacob groaned long and low. Ian hummed over his cock. Moaning and swaying to the rhythm of his sucking, Jacob let Ian know how much he liked it. But then he warned Ian, "Don't get carried away."

He took hold of Ian's face and gently pushed him back while watching his cock pop out of his mouth. He ran his thumb over Ian's lips while his blue eyes shone with desire. He stepped toward the bed and pulled his shirt and pants and boxers off. Still kneeling, Ian watched mesmerized as his amazing body was revealed.

"Get up," Jacob told him gruffly.

Ian could have kneeled at his feet, worshiping him forever with his mouth and his eyes. As Ian stood up, Jacob sat on the edge of his bed and pulled him into his lap. Ian breathed hard as he explored Jacob with a light touch. That firm body, chiseled and hard under his hands was a dream.

"This is all mine," Ian said as he ran his hands all over him from his chest down to his abs and over his thighs – everything hard and muscled, perfect.

Jacob groped his ass, squeezing and digging his fingers in. "I feel the same way about this."

Ian bit his shoulder. "Then you better take it before I eat you alive."

Jacob growled and grazed his neck with his teeth. He grabbed lube out of the nightstand and slicked up his fingers. Then Ian was in for more torture.

As he fingered him for a long time, Jacob nuzzled his neck. "Are you ready for me?" Jacob asked cruelly.

"I'm ready to tear you to pieces if you don't fuck me," Ian threatened even as he writhed on his lap, taking his fingers and trying not to come.

Jacob's hand groped down his body. Reaching his cock, he grabbed hold and rubbed it carelessly. He treated Ian's body like he owned it. Sucking Jacob's tongue deep into his mouth,

Ian thrust into his hand. It wasn't enough.

Kissing his jaw, Jacob scraped his stubble over Ian's. "Tell me what you need," Jacob whispered harshly in his ear.

"You," Ian said before he could even think. He wanted to say "fuck me". But some more truthful part of him said, "I need you."

Ian pushed back from Jacob so he could see him. He was a sight. The intensity in his eyes was frightening. Groaning with need, looking at Ian like he wanted to rip into him, he was unbelievably hot.

With the condom on, Jacob pulled him forward and Ian leaned back. He had a bruising grip on Jacob's shoulders as he impaled himself on his cock. Inch by inch, he pushed down, taking him in. Jacob's cock was a dream, but Ian had to go easy or be split open.

Jacob must have lost patience with him. He flipped him over and down on the bed. Ian raised his legs to hook them around his back as Jacob shoved back in. Ian wanted to show him he wasn't a wimp. He pushed his hips up, taking Jacob's cock deeper.

Maybe he was a wimp. For a moment, he was so overwhelmed, he could only gasp and writhe. It was already too much when Jacob thrust one final time pushing all the way in. As Jacob filled him completely, Ian moaned and whimpered.

"I got you now," he said to Jacob. "I own you."

"Fine by me," Jacob told him. He lowered his head and kissed him deep and hard.

It was one of those breath-stealing kisses that pushed Ian right through the mattress. Jacob was getting ready to show him that he owned him just as much. As the kiss went on, Jacob's body was hard against his, not letting him move. Ian needed to move. He needed to make something happen.

The pressure inside him was unbearable. He would burst. He

would die. "Please," he begged Jacob.

Satisfied by that one magic word, Jacob pulled back then thrust in.

Ian's back arched off the bed and he gasped. So this was what Jacob was after. He wanted to split him open with one long, deep thrust. It sent Ian right out of his mind.

"Thank you. Oh, God. Yes," Ian heard himself gasp. When this was over, he was going to make Jacob pay for making him say that. For now, he was just grateful for every hard punch of Jacob's cock inside him.

Pressing down on the backs of Ian's thighs, he started fucking Ian hard enough to shake the bed, the room and Ian's whole world. Ian was crying out louder all the time. He felt helpless, rising all the time toward a climax that would shatter him.

His body clenched and Jacob cursed as Ian called his name. Ian came with a yell that ripped out of his throat. Then with one hand on Jacob's ass and another on the back of his neck, he stared up at him, ready for him to come. Blue eyes like ice, jaw clenched, Jacob looked down at him and slammed into him.

"You're mine," Ian told him and Jacob came with the shudder and a roar.

"I like the things I've discovered about you," Ian said as he and Jacob sprawled on his bed. They had cleaned up but they were still naked.

"Like what?" Jacob's hand was lazily mussing his hair as Ian lay on his chest.

Ian raised his head to look at him. "That you fuck like a maniac," he said with a satisfied grin.

"I can't seem to help myself," Jacob said with a slight frown, like he wasn't proud of his performance.

Ian kissed him. "It wasn't a complaint. But I'll look forward to whatever you'll do to me when we have plenty of time."

Jacob's smile was full of evil promises. He gave Ian a long, deep kiss that drove him wild, but he broke it off before things got out of hand.

Ian untangled himself from Jacob. "Don't kiss me like that when I have to go."

"I told you I can't help it. I only want to do bad things to you," Jacob said as he ogled Ian while he was bent over picking up his clothes.

"I don't believe that for a second," Ian told him as he pulled on his jeans. "You're a good guy with a big heart."

Jacob climbed out of bed too and started putting his own clothes back on. He looked thoughtful, like maybe he still had some doubts about the two of them. Ian walked over and hooked his arm around Jacob's neck.

"Did you already forget you're mine?" Ian said while staring into his eyes. "I meant what I said. I don't blurt out just anything while I fuck."

Ian kissed him hard, showing him what he could do, that he could steal his breath and his soul if he wanted to. But even when he acted brave, he was so scared. He was no match for Jacob. Ian was in his power. His chest tightened painfully whenever he saw doubt in Jacob's beautiful eyes. His whole world threatened to spin out of control. Despite his show of confidence, one look, one word from Jacob could crush him.

CHAPTER 17

*I*an wished he could spend all his time convincing Jacob they were meant to be together, but they both had other worries taking up their time. With this thorny issue of Lorna between them, Ian still tried not to be angry with his dad. He was too worried about his health. The last thing he wanted to do was make things harder on his dad when he was suffering and fighting for his life.

He did his best to act normal and not to betray his obsession with what he had found out. But hearing Lorna speak to him didn't only give him a clue about who he was, it also unearthed something from his memory. Over the last few nights, Ian had woken up from dreams of what happened when he was a kid and he jumped over the fence at number 211.

As usual these days, he really wanted to talk to Jacob about it. Actually he just wanted to see him and be with him all the time. When they were apart, he ached. The longing was constant like Jacob was now a part of him.

While his dad rested, Ian went to town and walked around aimlessly. It was midday Sunday and quite a few people were strolling around. Standing in front of Heartstone's Bakery, Ian smelled something fresh baked. He went in to check it out and called up Jacob.

"Can I invite myself over for lunch?"

"Sure. Come over," Jacob said.

"Great. I'm standing in the bakery, and the Kaiser rolls just came out of the oven."

"Bring them over. I think we have everything else we need."

When Ian arrived at Jacob's with two bags in his arms, Toby opened the door to him.

"I knew it was you," Toby said excitedly. "You knock two times then one time. And Dad told me you were coming."

Ian laughed at his detective work. "I wanted to hang out with you guys. And look what I brought." Ian showed him the two heirloom tomatoes he had gotten along with the fresh buns. "Funny looking aren't they? They're from the greenhouse at Mr. Brewer's."

Seeing the two tomatoes, Toby didn't look pleased.

"Don't you like tomatoes?" Ian asked.

Toby shook his head.

"Tomatoes are good."

"You eat them," Toby said as he led the way to the kitchen.

"I will. But I want you to have some too. You should like tomatoes. Tomatoes are what ketchup is made from," Ian said as he put the bags down on the kitchen counter.

"No!" Toby said, shocked by this news.

"Yes. Why do you think there's a tomato on the label?" Ian said as he pulled a bottle of ketchup from the fridge as well as other sandwich fixings.

Toby shrugged. Ian turned over the bottle of ketchup to show Toby the label on the back.

"Read the ingredients. See, it says tomatoes."

"I can't read," Toby said.

"Then you'll have to take my word for it. You can't hate tomatoes if you like ketchup," Ian told him.

Toby looked very conflicted. When his dad came into the kitchen, he told him the shocking thing he had just learned about where ketchup comes from.

"You never mentioned that to him?" Ian asked Jacob.

"I didn't want to ruin ketchup for him."

"Don't be crazy. Nothing can ruin ketchup," Ian told him.

Seeing him rummaging through his refrigerator, Jacob asked, "Can I help you find something?"

"You said you had everything, I don't see pepperoni," Ian complained.

"Yes. We should have pepperoni," Toby agreed.

"I didn't realize pepperoni was an essential ingredient for making a sandwich. Maybe a pizza," Jacob said as he started slicing the rolls.

"Can we have pizza?" Toby asked.

"Stock up on some pepperoni for next time. It doesn't just go on pizza. Toby would like pepperoni on his sandwich, right?" Ian said and looked at Toby.

Toby nodded. They were in agreement about pepperoni, but he still wasn't sold on the tomatoes. As Ian and Jacob made sandwiches, Toby eyed the tomato slices anxiously. His love of ketchup won the day, and he said OK to one paper thin tomato slice going into his sandwich. Ian put a glob of ketchup right on the tomato slice to make it go down easier.

After lunch, Ian asked Jacob to step into the back garden with him.

"So why are we here? Did you want to try and talk to her again?" Jacob wondered.

Ian stared around and tried to think back to what the place used to look like when he was a boy. "Just refreshing my memory. I think there's something that makes us forget seeing ghosts as kids?"

"Oh?"

"Something came back to me. When I was a kid, I had a scary experience in this garden."

"It came back to you?"

"I remembered some of it all along – climbing into the garden. I remembered being spooked by something and running away. I didn't remember what happened between the time I climbed over the fence and when I started running. I thought it was just a noise or something that scared me. But hearing Lorna's voice brought it back. I realized that wasn't the first time she spoke to me."

"What did she say?"

"Something that makes sense to me only now. Kind of."

When he was eight, the garden wasn't the way it was now. The house had been sitting abandoned for years. The garden was a mess. Everything was growing wild and out of control. Once Ian was over the fence and in the midst of it, all he could see was green.

At first, Ian was both scared and curious. But the deeper he went, the more he felt cut off from what he left behind, from his friends, from everything real. He walked in a straight line, but the way back didn't seem clear to him.

After only a few steps, nothing around him was the same. It got dark. He didn't know where all the sunshine went so fast. It was so cold and the air was too thick. The shadows were menacing, crowding in on him. He didn't know which way to run.

He couldn't hear anything, not the birds, or the wind in the branches, or cars passing on the street. His friends weren't calling out to each other any more. Everything was taken away until the world was a black silence. He was swallowed up.

Next to him, the darkness shifted, threatening to change shape. As he stood frozen, he could hear it breathing. The sound got louder until it was as loud as a storm. The noise pushed him down. He wanted to curl up into a ball.

Then he heard a sound of splintering and he saw a patch of light. The shape it made was jittery, but he thought it was sort of like a woman. He kept his eyes on her, afraid to look away. At least she was bright even if her light was cold and flickering like it was close to burning out.

She was coming closer. Ian didn't want that, but he couldn't move. A rasping sound filled his ears, coming from too close to him even if there was nothing there.

Ian saw her coming closer all the time but never arriving. He couldn't make her out. Then she tried to speak. Her words were far away, and at first they didn't make any sense. Suddenly, she winked out and Ian was alone in a deathly still blackness. Then inside the darkness there was a voice. Low and rasping, cutting in and out, it said to him, "You left me alone."

How he got out, how he climbed the fence, Ian didn't know. He just remembered running away, his lungs hurting. He was running full out until he got home. For weeks he had to sleep with the lights on, but he didn't tell his parents why.

After Ian finished telling him what happened to him, Jacob looked grim.

"What happened to your theory that kids are more attuned to ghosts and have a friendlier relationship with them?" he asked.

"I guess that doesn't apply to me," Ian said. He didn't really understand it. "I wasn't just any kid. She knew who I was then, and she blamed me for leaving her alone, for living when she died."

"You think she blames you for that?" Jacob asked. It was obvious he found it hard to believe, maybe because he was a parent.

"I don't think we can expect a ghost to be sane and reasonable," Ian pointed out.

"I'm still struggling with the fact that they exist," Jacob said.

"Too late for that." Ian looked at him and wondered if he was the most pigheaded person on the planet or what.

"It can't be easy knowing that she's your mother," Jacob said.

"And that she hates me. But she seems to have found a substitute in Toby."

"My Toby is the sweetest boy in the world. But I wish she hadn't taken a shine to him."

"Especially when the real thing is right here. Does she still blame me like before or maybe she doesn't even recognize me?" Ian wondered. "And God knows how my deadbeat, biological father is going to react to seeing me. Not to mention he's the most likely suspect in her death. How messed up is that?"

"If you're determined to see him..."

"I am. I have to do this."

"I wasn't trying to talk you out of it. I want to come with you," Jacob said.

That was unexpected and really great of him. "This is what separates a good boyfriend from a boyfriend that's getting woken up with a blowjob for the rest of his life."

Jacob grumbled then tried to minimize his awesome gesture. "It's not a big deal. I can call in sick."

Ian smiled at him. "OK. I think that would be good. I feel like I have too many things coming at me all at once."

"You do," Jacob agreed and pulled him into a hug.

"You know you're worth knowing just for the hug benefits. Everything else is just gravy."

"My sexual prowess is not flattered."

Ian pulled away and smiled. "I promise to flatter you later."

CHAPTER 18

*M*onday, Jacob came to pick him up around noon. His Toyota 4runner was a bigger car than he needed, strictly speaking. Ian wondered if he was planning to have a whole bunch of kids to fill up this car. It made him smile to think of a whole bunch of little Jacob clones chattering in the back.

They got on the highway and the ride was smooth. Sitting next to Jacob, Ian was tense but he could still enjoy the feeling of being with him. If this was an ordinary drive, he would have had his hands all over him.

Preoccupied with a confrontation that might not even happen, Ian stared out the window and worried. The sky was very blue in the distance, but low, gray clouds with ragged edges passed overhead. To their left, Mapleview was coming into view.

"Whenever we drove by here, a friend of mine used to ask, 'Who do you have to kill to live there?' Now I'm thinking the answer is your pregnant girlfriend," Ian said bitterly.

"You don't know that."

"No, but there isn't a long list of suspects, and most of them have the last name Dufresne."

From the highway, Mapleview looked like a picaresque little town of mansion surrounded by the serene beauty of miles of golf courses. There was no way to get in without going through a well-guarded gate. That's why they were passing it up and going to Lambton and to Newacre Real Estate headquarters instead.

Lambton benefited a great deal from being so close to Mapleview. They got a lot of spillover. People who couldn't quite afford Mapleview lived there. Everything was a little more polished and high-end, including the office buildings.

Jacob parked his car on the street right in front of Newacre Real Estate headquarters. Getting inside their high-rise office building would have been a challenge, but waiting outside wasn't a problem. Jacob stayed in the car and Ian got out. He walked up the sidewalk and hung around, but not so close to the building that he would attract attention from security.

He kept an eye on the front steps of the building so he could approach Dufresne as soon as he came out. He knew what he looked like from his internet search. Past the steps, he could see the entrance to the parking garage. There was a gate and a security guard on duty.

Ian was pretty sure he didn't need to watch for Dufresne coming from there. He had already noticed four executive cars waiting outside in the short, circular driveway. Ian was willing to bet that one of them was waiting for Kurt Dufresne.

That turned out to be a bad bet. Ten minutes later, Ian saw several people get into the waiting cars, and none of them were Dufresne. Where the hell was he? Maybe he never even came to the meeting. Ian's heart was sinking.

Looking around frantically, Ian saw Dufresne just as he was pulling out of the garage in a black sports car. Ian signaled to Jacob to follow the car. Jacob looked like he was about to make a turn to pick him up, but Ian motioned for him to keep going and follow Dufresne.

Watching the sports car then Jacob's car disappear down the street, Ian started walking in that same direction. Maybe Dufresne was just going home. If he didn't stop somewhere, this was all a big a waste of time. A few minutes later, Jacob called.

"He's at Juniper's. It's a bar four blocks straight up the street from where I left you, then one block right. Do you want me to come pick you up?"

"No. I'm halfway there. Stay and make sure he doesn't leave. I'll be there soon." Ian started running. Thanks to Jacob, they had him.

Juniper's was a fancy bar. The décor was ultra modern and the lighting had an obnoxious, icy shine. Ian wasn't sure he could afford a drink there even if he wasn't too young to buy one. Not to mention he didn't fit their customer profile. Running there hadn't done anything to make him look more presentable. Huffing a little and looking scruffy, Ian expected he might get kicked out of the place.

No one paid attention to him though, not even Dufresne as he sat at one of the tables and looked out the windows. That gave Ian a chance to look him over.

Growing up, Ian was always aware that he didn't look like his parents. He didn't look like the pictures of Lorna Hayes he had seen either. She had honey blond hair and hazel eyes. She was pretty, but not spectacularly beautiful or anything.

The pictures of Dufresne had already clued him in. This man was who he looked like – furry eyebrows, dark blue eyes, thick brown hair that couldn't be tamed if it grew longer than an inch. While Ian let his hair grow wild, Dufresne had brought his under control. It was cut short and slicked back with some product.

Even with him sitting down, Ian could tell Dufresne was taller than him. He wasn't thin either. He had the body of a jock gone soft. There was something lazy and ingratiating about him, like he was born to sell cars and he had missed out on his calling by marrying rich.

Ian went up to him and stood over him. He didn't bother with small talk.

"I'm Ian Warwick. That name wouldn't mean anything to you, but Lorna Hayes was my birthmother. Word is that you're my father," Ian said then waited for him to react.

Dufresne stood up. As he did, he kind of towered over Ian. Stunned, he looked Ian up and down.

"You are, aren't you," he said while staring at Ian closely. He then grabbed him by the shoulders.

"Hey," Ian protested. He tried to pull away from him, but instead of letting go Dufresne drew him into a hug.

It was so unexpected, Ian just stood there. It was a much better reception than he had expected, but he couldn't exactly return the hug while wondering if the man had killed his mother.

Once Dufresne let him go, he and Ian sat down. Ian was unnerved by how he stared at him and smiled, like he couldn't believe his eyes.

"Mr. Dufresne..."

"You can call me Kurt, if you want," he said tentatively.

"Let me be clear. I'm not here because I want anything from you except answers. I'm all set when it comes to parents," Ian told him.

"Are they good to you?" Kurt asked.

Ian just stared at him for a minute. "Timely question, twenty years after you wrote me off. Yes, they're good to me. They're great parents. But I want to know about you and Lorna."

For the first time, Kurt looked away from him. He stared at his drink, which he hadn't touched since Ian arrived. Now he picked it up and downed the whole glass.

"I met my wife, my future wife. That's what happened. I could see my whole life so clearly. Lorna wasn't in it. Or you. I dumped her. I told her I'd give her money for... the baby, but she didn't want it."

Ian could guess that he must have offered her money for an abortion.

"Did you come to Blystone to see her?" Ian asked though he didn't expect him to tell the truth.

Kurt shook his head. "The last time I talked to her was at school."

"I'm not asking if you talked to her. I'm asking if you came by and killed her?"

Kurt slumped back and shook his head again. He didn't say anything, but he did stare at Ian with a hurt look.

Ian pressed on. "The police didn't find any evidence that you arranged to meet. I'm thinking you drove to Blystone and you just happen to see her on the side of the road. You either had a fight or you just saw your chance to be rid of her and you offed her."

"I wasn't there. I was with my friends," Kurt said, sounding tired.

"Friends lie."

"I didn't kill her. That accusation is always going to hang over me. But you have to believe me. I didn't hurt her," Kurt said and reached out across the table as if he would put his hands on Ian again.

Ian drew back. "What about your father or someone else in your family?"

"My mother and father were in the Caribbean at the time."

"Then it comes back to you." Ian stood up. "Since you want me to believe you, you think you can arrange a meeting between me and the friends who were with you that night?"

"Dave is in Japan, but you can call him. I'll tell him to take your call. But I'm afraid Neil died in a plane crash five years ago."

The only guy he could talk to was still chummy with Kurt. Ian could already hear him repeating Kurt's alibi from years ago. Ian sighed bitterly and turned to walk away.

"Wait. How do I keep in touch with you?" Kurt asked.

Ian turned back to him, incredulous. Kurt had stood up and he was reaching for Ian again. Ian made sure to stay out of his reach.

"You don't. Unless you have something new to tell me?" Ian asked.

Wearing that hurt look, Kurt only shook his head, and Ian walked out.

On the drive back, Ian gave Jacob the short version of meeting Kurt. He was tired of the whole thing, and really, there wasn't much to say. He didn't find out anything new.

After giving him a kiss, Jacob dropped him off in front of the house. It was around four in the afternoon, but Ian felt like it was much later. That pointless meeting with Kurt had taken more out of him than he expected. As he came through the front door, Ian found his father standing in the living room. He was hunched over, out of breath, leaning heavily on the back of the couch.

"Are you OK? Where's Mrs. Astor?" Ian asked as he took hold of him.

His father's words came out haltingly. "I sent her home."

"Are you feeling nauseous?" Ian asked then he smelled booze. "Dad, you aren't supposed to drink."

On the coffee table, he saw a bottle of scotch sitting next to a glass.

"Can't even drink the way I used to. Can't do anything right," his dad lamented.

"Don't talk like that," Ian told him.

Taking his dad's arm to steady him, he led him toward the front of the couch.

"I never did anything. I'm dying and I never did anything good in my life, not one good thing. Nothing." His dad gasped out the words.

"Come and sit here." Ian lowered him to the couch gently as he told him, "You did plenty. You have your work and you've been a great dad."

"No," his dad protested and turned away from him.

"Yes, you have. Now try and settle down. You're OK. Everything is OK."

"I don't feel good."

"That's because you're not supposed to drink," Ian told him. He sat down on the couch with his dad. Putting his arms around him, he encouraged him to lean against him. "We'll just sit here and everything will be OK."

With his head on Ian's shoulder, his dad told him, "You're a good son. I wish I was a good dad to you."

"You are." Ian put his arm around him tighter feeling how very thin he was.

It didn't take long for his dad to lean back and fall asleep right there on the couch. Ian sat with him until it got dark.

CHAPTER 19

A few hours later, Ian went into town. His dad's words bothered him. Why did he think he didn't do anything good? Plus his meeting with Kurt weighed on him. He couldn't do anything about his dad or Kurt, but maybe he could sort out this thing with Lorna and give Jacob and Toby some peace.

Stepping up to Jacob's door, he knocked very lightly. He figured Toby must be asleep by now, and he didn't want to disturb him.

"Are you OK?" Jacob asked him as soon as he opened the door.

"I guess," Ian said, not sure how to answer. He went in and tried to explain why he was there. "I left my dad asleep. I wanted to come over here and try something. I want to see if I can talk to Lorna. Maybe I can get her to tell me what it will take for her to leave Toby alone." Ian knew he sounded worked up and kind of crazy.

Jacob frowned at him as they stood in the front hall. "You look tired. Don't you want to get some sleep yourself? You can do this tomorrow."

"No. I don't want to wait. I read online that it's better to try and contact spirits at night. And I'd rather do this with Toby in bed, asleep. I don't want him caught in the middle if it gets unpleasant."

"You expect it to get unpleasant?" Jacob asked.

Ian shook his head. "I don't know. She seemed hostile to me before. It's like she knows who I am, but she doesn't know what it means. I'm thinking that if I can get her to fully recognize that I'm her son, it might fix things."

Jacob sighed and then nodded. They went through to the kitchen. Jacob took a seat at the kitchen table and Ian stepped outside.

The light from above the back door was shining into the garden as well as the one from the street. The treetops still had enough leaves left to swallow some of that light. Ian took a deep breath of the cold, night air. He didn't really feel up to an encounter with Lorna, but he just needed to do something.

Not sure he was ready, he walked toward the bench. He didn't see anything, but the chilly air suddenly got freezing cold. Ian felt pressure in his ears and then a splintering sound that turned to the familiar rushing noise. It seemed worse than before and he was only able to breathe with a lot of effort.

"Do you know who I am?" he asked. It was like he was shouting into the wind that was stealing his breath.

He kept looking around for her, but he didn't see anything, only darkness. That's when he realized that the garden had turned almost black. That was a sure sign that she was there.

"Why don't you answer me?" he demanded.

The darkness in front of him thickened. He felt something very close and he felt dizzy. The whooshing noise in his ears got unbearably loud. Then she spoke. Rather than breaking through the rushing sound, her voice was woven into it. Ian could barely make out the words.

"You stink like the man who killed me."

Ian couldn't hear clearly, but he was sure that was what she said. He tried to speak, to ask her to confirm it, but he couldn't. For a moment he saw a bright blue shape. Then it was over.

The pressure, the noise, the chill, they were all gone. Ian slumped to the ground panting and Jacob came out of the house and ran over to him. Pulling Ian to his feet, he looked at him closely. He took his hands and rubbed them to warm him up.

"Did you hear her?" Ian asked. He was staring around him and blinking. Back the way it was, the garden looked strange to him.

"No. She said something?" Jacob asked, squeezing Ian's hands in his own.

Ian stopped staring and turned to Jacob. "Yes. She said I smelled like her killer. That means it was Kurt Dufresne." Ian was surprised. He had almost convinced himself that he didn't do it. Kurt didn't seem to him like someone who could kill a pregnant girl. The realization that he killed Lorna hit Ian hard.

"You can't be sure that's what it means," Jacob told him.

"But I am. Why did she say that only today. Because when I went to see Kurt, he hugged me. That's when his smell got on me. His cologne was pretty strong. She must have recognized it."

"Cologne? He can't possibly wear the same cologne he wore twenty years ago," Jacob said reasonably.

"I don't know. But she said it. She said he killed her."

"What are you going to do?" Jacob asked as he put an arm around him and led him inside.

"Right now, go home, make sure my dad is OK. I'll figure out what to do about Kurt tomorrow. I can't even think right now, but I know an accusation from a ghost isn't something I can take to the police. I'm going to have to look for proof. Now I better go see about my dad. He's in worse shape than ever."

"I'm sorry."

"I stressed him out. He was drinking."

"You're taking on too much, guilt and everything. Just go home and sleep," Jacob told him. He sent him home with a kiss.

Ian found his dad sitting up on the couch. He looked pale and weak, but more like himself.

Ian went over to take a closer look at him. "How are you feeling?"

"Are you OK?" his dad asked, ignoring his question.

Feeling heavy and tired, Ian sat down next to him. "Not great. I found out Kurt Dufresne killed Lorna. She was in the way, and I was too. He tried to get rid of both of us. He killed her, and I'm going to prove it," Ian said. The knowledge made him sick and angry too. He couldn't let him get away with it.

"No. Leave it alone," his dad said and grabbed his arm.

"What do you mean 'leave it alone'? No. I can't. I'm going after him. The man murdered her."

"He didn't. It wasn't him." His dad squeezed his arm then let it go.

Ian turned to him more fully. "How do you know?"

His dad closed his eyes tightly, then he spoke. "It was me."

It was only a hoarse whisper. Ian wasn't sure he heard him right. He felt his temples throb and his heart thumped slowly but loudly. "What?"

"I killed Lorna, but it was an accident. It was dark. She was walking on the side of the road. I was driving home. I was drunk. It was dark and I didn't see her."

Hearing all that, Ian thought he might throw up. "You ran her over?"

"I didn't. I never actually hit her. I had trouble staying on the road. I kept veering off. I didn't see her and I got too close to her. She tried to get out of the way and fell. She fell into the ditch and hit her head on a rock."

"Did you drove away?" Ian asked, He dreaded hearing the answer.

"No. I got out of the car and went to her. She was barely conscious. Then she started going into labor. I didn't know what to do. I couldn't leave her. Son, I saw you being born."

"And then what?"

"I was afraid to move her. And I didn't know what to do about the umbilical cord. Even if I knew, I was too drunk. I didn't trust myself to do anything. I went to call for help."

"You left."

"I had to. My phone hardly ever had a signal. I couldn't move her or you. I put you in her arms. I didn't know what else to do. I went to the payphone at the bus stop. I called for an ambulance. Then..." His father went silent.

Ian finished for him. "You left her to die."

"I didn't. I called for help."

"Did you go back to check on her, to be with her?"

"No. I couldn't. I was driving drunk."

"Oh, God." Ian leaned forward. Now he was sure he would throw up. This was what Lorna meant. Booze from his father's drinking binge earlier – that was the smell she was talking about. It must have gotten on Ian when he held him before. That's the smell she recognized from that night. The man who killed her.

"I'm sorry. I'm so sorry," his father said, but Ian heard him only distantly.

"You adopted me out of guilt," Ian realized.

"I couldn't stop thinking about you. When your great-grandmother got sick, I just wanted to take care of you."

"And Mom? Did Mom know about all this?"

"No. But eventually I had to tell her the truth. It's the reason she divorced me. When you turned fifteen, she wanted to tell you about your birthmother. That's when I finally told her the truth about what I had done. After that, she couldn't even look at me."

"Mom took me to the memorial around that time, right before she moved. She said she just wanted to take a walk, but she had me take along a small white rose in a planter. She said she wanted to leave it at the memorial since she was moving away. But she made me put it there, and asked me to take care of it. The rose died during the winter." Ian thought about that unstable metal contraption. "The memorial? Who put it up?"

"I'm afraid I did more drinking after the night Lorna died. One night, I went to the spot. I saw all the flowers and trinkets people were leaving for her. I remembered the stand we had in the cellar, buried under a bunch of old junk. I don't know what it was for, but it had shelves. I got it out and took it to the spot where she died. It wouldn't have stood all these years, but someone put spikes into the ground to hold it up. Someone else attached a wooded plaque with her name, but that's gone now."

For a while, they sat in silence broken only by his dad's coughing and his ragged breathing. Ian wondered if his dad had anything to eat since the little bit he got down for breakfast. Ian stood up, not sure he could stand and not fall, but he did. He heard his father make a strangled noise.

Ian turned to him. His head was down and his shoulders were shaking.

"I'll be right back. I'll bring you a breakfast bar and some tea. You need to eat something."

Ian flipped on the light in the kitchen. It was incredibly painful to his eyes, but he couldn't see without it. He had trouble remembering where the breakfast bars were. At first he couldn't hold the teapot. His hands were shaking so hard, they were useless. He got them under control a little, and poured the lukewarm tea a little at a time so he wouldn't spill it. Then he went back to his dad.

He still couldn't raise his head.

"You're going to eat and drink this, for me," Ian told him.

His dad looked up. His eyes were wet and he was shaking.

"You need to eat," Ian told him and made him sit up.

Putting the breakfast bar in his hand, Ian watched him while he ate. His dad could only eat one small bite at a time. After every bite, Ian handed him the cup with the tea. He had to steady his hand so he wouldn't spill it. When he was done, Ian put him to bed. Then he stayed up until he just couldn't keep his eyes open any more.

Ian woke up in the armchair across from his father's bed. It was early morning. His dad was standing over him, touching his hair.

"You always did have a lot of it," his dad said. "You should go to bed now."

Ian started crying. He didn't mean to. He just couldn't hold it in any more. As quickly as he could manage to get himself under control, he stopped and breathed. His dad had leaned down to hug him. He kissed the top of his head and then smoothed down his hair.

"I'm so sorry, Ian."

CHAPTER 20

*A*fter his confession, things between him and his dad were strained. Ian had to muzzle himself and hold back everything he wanted to say. If his dad wasn't so sick, Ian might have raged, moved out, refused to see him.

All of that was out of the question. His dad was fighting for every breath. He could hardly take one step without help, and he used the oxygen tank more than ever before. Even when Mrs. Astor was there, Ian hated to leave him. His dad had to beg him to get out of the house.

"Go see your friend," he told Ian.

Ian finally listened. As he took a walk to Jacob's house, he stopped in front of Lorna's memorial.

"I'm sorry," he said to her. "My dad is sorry too. He really is."

His words hung in the air. He looked and listened, but there was nothing to see or hear. The wind did pick up for a moment, and Ian held his breath, but nothing happened. It was just a cool evening on the side of the road.

Ian looked down at his feet. He was born here. Did his cries fill the night as his mother was dying? As much as he wished his dad had come back to the scene and accepted responsibility for what he did, Ian didn't want to erase his whole life. His mom and dad loved him without a doubt. Even knowing what his dad did and what his mom kept from him, he still loved them.

It was late evening by the time he was standing on Jacob's doorstep. When Jacob opened the door he was wiping his hands with a kitchen towel.

"I was just doing dishes? Dinner is still warm, you want some?"

"No, thanks," Ian said. Seeing Jacob, he felt like his heart would burst. His eyes were so blue. Even as he frowned at Ian worriedly, he was beautiful. Ian just wanted to tell him, "Hold me and make everything go away."

Jacob stared at him. He could tell something was wrong. After letting Toby say hi to him, Jacob sent him to his room to do his homework.

That left them alone to talk. Sitting on Jacob's couch, Ian didn't know how to get the words out. He was numb. Underneath that, his head was full of so many contradictions he just wanted to scream. After a few false starts, everything spilled out of him.

Once Ian was done speaking, he just breathed for a while, nothing more. That's when he found that Jacob was holding him. How had that happened?

"I guess I'm kind of out of it," Ian said, pulling back.

"I'm so sorry," Jacob told him.

"I look at my dad, and I just can't see the man responsible for Lorna's death. I just see my dad. I should hate him for what he did. But he is so sick. I'm too afraid of losing him to hate him," Ian said.

"No one is asking you to hate him," Jacob told him.

Ian disagreed. "I think Lorna is. The way she sees it, my dad killed her and then he stole her child."

"You can't hate your dad because a ghost wants you to," Jacob said, always so rational.

That's when Toby ran in.

"Ian can watch cartoons with us!" he said excitedly.

"I guess you're done with your homework," Jacob said.

Toby nodded then came to sit between them.

Ian watched TV with Jacob and Toby for a while. They talked about what costume Toby was going to wear for Halloween. He was going to be a Ninja Turtle, specifically Leonardo.

"You should come trick-or-treating with us. But you have to wear a costume or you won't get any candy," Toby told him.

Ian wasn't making any promises about a costume, but he did tell Toby which houses had the good candy.

After everything he learned about his family, it did him so much good just to sit with Jacob and Toby like that. No secrets, no confessions, just love.

Then it was Toby's bedtime, and he was left alone with Jacob again. Ian leaned against him, and Jacob pulled him into a hug. With Jacob's arms around him, leaning his face against his shoulder, Ian felt so good.

"Are you going to be OK?" Jacob asked him.

"Not for a while," Ian told him honestly. Except for Jacob and Toby, he didn't see anything good ahead. That's why he said to Jacob, "I can't stop thinking about you. But I'm afraid you might forget me as soon as I'm gone."

"Are you going somewhere?" Jacob's voice had an edge to it.

"Back to school at some point," Ian said.

"Oh, OK. You had me worried. I already miss you every second you're gone. If you left, really left, I would chase you down to the ends of the earth," Jacob said, speaking in a deep, earnest whisper.

For a moment, Ian was too breathless to speak. "You could have told me. I wasn't sure how you felt. All this time I've been playing it cool."

"When was this exactly?" Jacob asked.

Ian tilted his head up to see an ironic look in his eyes. "Don't try to score off me. You don't know cool. I'm surprised I'm even into a stick in the mud guy like you."

"And the compliments just keep coming. You know I'll make you pay for saying crap like that." Now the look in his eyes was positively deadly.

Ian could say only one thing to a threat like that, "You can do whatever you want to me. I'm all yours."

"Are you?" As he asked the question, the intensity in his gaze startled Ian.

"If you want me to be."

"I'm dead serious. Can you say the same thing?" Jacob asked sternly. Damn, that was one scary, hot expression he was wearing.

"Yes. When I'm with you, I feel like my soul is on fire and my bones are melting. That's what you do to me. Even if you didn't want me, I would be yours forever."

Jacob gave him a slow smile. Then he grabbed him by the back of the head and gave him a deep kiss. A low moan traveled between them from mouth to mouth. Ian took only one moment to breathe and said, "I love you" before he went back to kissing Jacob.

He rubbed his hands over Jacob's short hair while Jacob's fingers tangled in his. They kept their hands above the waist, clutching at each other's clothes but not daring to expose any skin. Out of breath, they pulled back to keep things from going too far with Toby sleeping just down the hall.

"You heard me say I love you, right?" Ian asked.

"I was busy, but yes, I heard," Jacob said coolly.

Ian punched his arm. "You don't need to say it back, but you do need to appreciate it."

"I love you too," Jacob said. He grinned at Ian and his eyes looked so happy.

While Ian stared at him wide-eyed, Jacob leaned over and kissed him. Ian couldn't believe that he said it, but that kiss didn't let him think. It hardly let him breathe. Jacob loved him.

CHAPTER 21

It was well past lunch time. Ian saw that his dad was still dozing. If his dad managed to sleep, Ian didn't like to wake him. But this time was different. Ian went up to him slowly.

Each step Ian took seemed to take an eternity. His legs were heavy. His heart was beating painfully slow, like it might stop. He put his hand on his dad's shoulder and really looked at him. With a shaking hand he searched for a pulse. Finally he placed his head on his chest. He stayed like that, listening for a long time even though there was nothing to hear.

His dad was gone. Ian straightened. He wanted to shout at him. He wanted to shake him awake. But he only sat down next to him and held his hand. He was gone. The thing he never wanted to face had happened. He had lost his dad.

There were painful phone calls and meaningless procedures to go through. It was all a blur until he was suddenly in Jacob's arms and he started sobbing uncontrollably.

Jacob held him for a long time, murmuring into his hair until Ian came back to himself. He barely remembered the stammering phone call he made to Jacob, telling him what had happened. Jacob would have still been at work. Ian realized he must have left work early. He was so grateful. Without his dad, the house was so empty and Ian felt so lost.

"His heart wasn't in good shape. The doctors were afraid of this," Ian told him when he was finally able to speak.

"I'm so sorry."

"Don't you have to pick up Toby?" Ian asked, seeing what time it was.

"I'll call Ruth and ask her to keep him a little while longer," Jacob said and got his phone out.

"I'm sorry. I was kind of out of it. I didn't realize what time it was. Go get him. I'll be OK," Ian told him.

"Why don't you come with me? You can stay over tonight," Jacob said, running his hands over Ian's arms.

"Thanks, but I think I want to stay here. I need to say goodbye to my dad. I don't know how to do that yet. I have to figure it out."

"If you're sure."

"I am. My mom is driving over. She'll be here soon."

Before leaving, Jacob told him, "Come over for breakfast then. Bring your mom."

"OK. I'll try."

*

Jacob hated to leave him there by himself, but he understood that he needed the time alone. He left Ian's house wishing he could take all his pain away. At the same time, he dreaded the task ahead of him once he got Toby home.

After dinner, he sat down with Toby and told him, "I have some bad news to tell you. Ian's dad died."

"His dad?" Toby frowned then shook his head. His bottom lip quivered. "No. Dads can't die," he said in a shaky voice then he burst into tears. Jacob held him and smoothed his hair. Toby raised his head from his shoulder. Through tears, he said, "You're never gonna die?"

"Not for a long time."

"No. Never. Promise," Toby demanded.

"It's natural to die."

"No."

"It is. Sorry," Jacob told him and kissed the top of his head.

That night Toby had trouble going to sleep. Jacob stayed with him even after he nodded off. He wanted to guard him from everything and make him every promise he needed to hear.

He also wished he could be with Ian to try and help him with what he was going through. One day soon, he might be able to be with his two favorite people at the same time. Ian wanted to share his life. When he first met him, it seemed impossible. Ian was too young. But since then, Ian had convinced him that a lot of crazy things were possible.

In the morning, Jacob made pancakes and Toby anxiously waited for Ian to arrive. When he texted he was on his way, Toby was beside himself. Jacob opened the door to Ian and hugged him right away.

"Ian!" Toby wailed when he came in. He ran up to him and looked up mournfully. "Your dad..." he started to say then he couldn't finish. He looked like he was going to cry.

Ian picked him up. Toby gulped a few tines but he didn't cry. If he had, Ian looked ready to burst into tears as well.

"You're a brave boy," Ian told him.

"No, I'm sad," Toby told him.

"Me too, but I'm glad you got to meet my dad."

Toby nodded. "He liked soup."

"Yes, he did. And he liked you and your dad too. He told me."

As Toby blinked back tears and Ian held him, Jacob rubbed his back.

"So what are we having for breakfast?" Ian asked to distract him from his sadness.

They went into the kitchen where the table was set with an extra place.

"You didn't bring your mom," Jacob said as he removed the forth plate.

"I asked her, but she said she didn't want to intrude. She stayed at the house. It's full of memories for her too. She does want to meet you and Toby. I showed her the picture of Toby with the drawing. She asked me if I had any of you. When I said I didn't, she asked 'Is your phone broken, honey?' She has found a lot of reasons to ask me that. She wants me texting her what I have for breakfast, lunch and dinner."

"Tell her we're having pancakes," Toby said helpfully as they all took their seats.

"I'll do better than that. I'm going to send her a picture of you eating a pancake, how's that?" Ian told him.

Toby posed with a stack of pancakes in front of him and a goofy smile on his face.

Ian got a text right after. Looking at his phone, he told Toby, "My mom said something scary. She said she could eat you for breakfast."

"What?" Toby said.

"Because you're so cute," Ian told him.

Now Toby looked shy. When Ian put away his phone and started eating, Toby eyed his plate disapprovingly.

"Your pancake is lonely all by itself. You have to have two," Toby told him.

"I didn't know there was a rule like that," Ian said.

"There is," Toby insisted.

Ian added another pancake and Toby smiled. Jacob knew he probably didn't feel like eating. When they were done eating and Toby left them alone, Jacob told Ian, "Thanks for making an effort for Toby."

"I don't have much of an appetite these days," Ian admitted. "I was eating mostly so I wouldn't worry my dad. Now I'll probably have to eat not to worry my mom."

"And you ate the second pancake for Toby's sake. I guess that's one way to keep you fed," Jacob said.

Ian was helping him clear the table, but Jacob took the plates out of his hands. Taking advantage of their moment of privacy, Jacob took him in his arms and tried to kiss every inch of his face. He wanted to kiss every inch of the rest of him too but that would have to wait.

"I didn't realize I would turn into such an idiot when I fell in love," Jacob whispered as he held Ian close.

"What's the problem?"

"I want to tell you I love you every second even when you're sad and just need to be held."

"That is terrible." Ian pulled back. "Haven't you been in love before?"

"No. I had some decent relationships, but I didn't know I could feel anything this painful and good except for Toby."

"Speak of the devil," Ian said as Toby came in.

Seeing how he almost caught them together, Jacob decided to bite the bullet.

"I forgot to tell you something," he said to Toby. "I have some good news. Ian is my boyfriend."

Toby gasped. Ian was almost as surprised. Toby came over to stare at Ian.

"You like my dad?" he asked.

"Yes. I like him a lot," Ian confirmed and grinned at Jacob.

Toby turned to Jacob. "Dad, he likes you." Jacob wished he didn't sound so surprised.

"Then he should definitely be my boyfriend," Jacob told him.

Toby nodded. He gave them both a big smile. "I like good news."

Ian and Jacob both hugged him.

"Go brush your teeth," Jacob told him.

Once he was gone, Ian came up to him. He put his arms around him. Letting one hand stroke through his hair and down the back of his neck, Ian kissed him.

"You made both of us smile. Thank you," he said, his eyes shining with happy tears.

Jacob placed his hands on his waist, slid them around and locked his arms behind him. "I should have told him before. And you too."

"No, this is perfect timing. Toby needed some happy news," Ian said.

Jacob had just leaned in for a kiss when Toby ran back into the kitchen.

Toby looked between them. "What does it mean? Now Ian is a boyfriend, what do we do?"

"We're going to do lots of stuff together," Ian told him.

"Like eat pancakes?" Toby said.

"Yes. And other fun stuff too."

"OK," Toby said and ran out again.

"He'll probably run out here with more questions," Jacob predicted.

"I better go before we end up engaged," Ian said with a sly smile.

"Yes, you better," Jacob teased him then gave him a kiss at the door.

"Thanks for finally admitting you're my boyfriend. I really liked hearing that." Ian got such a shy look on his face.

"I love you." Jacob couldn't help saying.

"You say the best stuff," Ian said and drew him closer. "I love you too." With those words and one last kiss he left.

Watching him go, Jacob knew that Ian had a lot more pain to go through. It was unavoidable, but he was determined to be there with him every step of the way.

CHAPTER 22

Cars were lined up outside the cemetery. People had gathered under yellow leaves and a sunny sky. Ian knew the place well. He used to play here. He and his friends would jump, climb over the headstones, sometimes try to scare each other.

Even with all the Warwick graves, including his grandparents', the cemetery was just another playground to him when he was a kid. Now it was one more place where he would try to say goodbye to his dad.

All this time knowing his dad probably wouldn't make it, and Ian wasn't able to even begin to let him go. He still couldn't. He felt that when he finally let his father go, something would break inside him forever.

Ian breathed through the pain in his chest as he tried not to cry. His mom was by his side and a good number of people had come from out of town for his father's funeral. As he looked around at all the mourners, Ian was surprised to see Jacob and Toby. Toby wore a shirt and tie under a blue, zipped jacket. He carried a small bunch of yellow flowers.

Jacob gave Ian a hug and then Ian crouched down to Toby's level. Toby moved to hug him then considered the flowers in his hand. Looking up at his dad, he handed the flowers to him for safekeeping. Then Toby wrapped his arms around Ian and leaned his head on his shoulder. As soon as he stepped back, he reached out for the flowers Jacob was holding for him.

"What do you have there?" Ian asked him.

"Flowers for your dad. Does he like yellow?" Toby asked in a hushed voice.

"Sure. He'll love them. Thank you."

Ian's mom stepped up to greet Jacob and Toby. They had already met her when they made a quick visit to the house. She was crazy about Toby. Until she met him, she had some reservations about Ian dating someone with a kid. Jacob made a good impression too.

"I pictured you with some scruffy guy with piercings and too much facial hair," she told Ian. "You did good, honey."

Now his mom was deep in conversation with Toby about who all the people were who had come for the funeral. A statue caught Toby's eye, and Ian's mom offered to take him over for a closer look. Ian knew she was just giving him a moment alone with Jacob.

"I'm surprised you brought Toby," Ian said. He knew Jacob was coming, but he thought Toby might be too young.

"I brought her," Jacob told him. The grim look on his face gave Ian a hint about who he meant.

"Lorna? You think..." Ian looked around as if he expected to see her appear out of thin air in this crowd and in broad daylight.

Jacob shook his head. "I don't know. But I told Toby to ask her to come. I hope that's OK."

"Maybe it will help. It's fine. I think." If it helped her to let go of her fixation on Toby, Ian was willing to try anything. His eyes darted around. He wondered if she could really be there. Finally he focused on Jacob. "Seeing you guys makes everything better. I think Toby is even cheering up my mom."

"He's my sweet boy." Jacob looked toward Toby, who was circling the statue of an old soldier leaning on a crutch. That's when he noticed who else was there.

"Isn't that...?" Jacob said as he recognized Kurt Dufresne standing apart from all the other mourners.

Ian had already noticed him. Kurt gave him a cautious smile but didn't approach him. Just as well. "Yeah. I can't believe he's here."

"Did you talk to him?"

"I'm not ready to deal with him," Ian said. He still felt like he might get crushed under the weight of everything he had found out and lost in such a short time.

Jacob squeezed his arm. "It's good that he came."

"I guess."

The service started soon after that, and Ian went to stand with his mom in front. Toby came to his other side and held his hand. Having that small hand in his own made Ian want to cry, but he held back his tears. Toby still had the yellow flowers in his other hand. Jacob stood close to him and kept his hand around his little shoulders, holding him close.

Ian didn't really hear anything that was said during the service. He only noticed when they started to lower the coffin into the ground. Once the grave was covered up, Jacob led Toby forward to place his flowers. Toby laid down the flowers with great care.

Watching him, Ian felt like he was seeing himself as a child giving his father one last token of his love. The little boy in Ian needed to say goodbye to his dad too. Then Jacob led Toby off to the side to give Ian and his mom a moment alone by the graveside.

As his mom took his hand, Ian suddenly felt his other hand get cold. He felt pressure as if cold fingers were squeezing his hand. Holding his breath, he heard a familiar noise like the rushing of the wind. The pressure on his hand eased, and he could swear he heard a woman's voice. It was pleasant but garbled. It faded, and the word "goodbye" formed within the rushing sound. Ian wondered if he had imagined it. Then everything went back to normal, and only one mom was holding his hand.

At the end of it, Ian found it hard to walk away. His feet felt rooted to the spot. He didn't want to leave his dad all alone. Telling himself he wasn't really there didn't seem to help.

Even as he stood over his grave, Ian wasn't sure where he should say goodbye to his dad. Here? In his study at the house where he sat for many hours working when he was well? At the window seat where he had spent so much time since he got sick? Nowhere. He didn't want to say goodbye at all. He couldn't.

"I'll be back to see you soon," he said to his dad, and he still barely managed to walk away.

CHAPTER 23

*I*an's mom had taken a few days off from work. Now it was time for her to go back home. The setting sun was turning the sky ruddy and the air cold. As he and his mom were standing by her car, saying goodbye, Ian pulled his jacket closer around him.

"I'm sorry you had to learn so many terrible things," his mom said.

"At least I'll be going forward with my eyes open." He didn't know how, but somehow he would just have to make peace with everything about his parents and who he was.

His mom touched his face and smiled sadly. "I wish your dad and I had a happier story to tell you. We just wanted to protect you. I still want to take all this pain away from you."

Ian could see how much she still wanted to protect him. "I can handle it," he assured her.

"My tough little guy," she said and squeezed him in a tight hug.

"Mom," Ian complained.

"You did get something good out of this. I'm glad you found that hunk and his little boy," she said as she took a step back.

"Instead of 'hunk', you could just call him Jacob," Ian told her.

"I just can't believe you're in such a serious relationship. You have grown up fast these last few months," she said with a sad but proud look in her eyes.

After she drove away, Ian locked the front door and went to Jacob's. While Jacob was making dinner, Ian found it impossible to stay out of the back garden. He walked out there while Toby hung out on the doorstep.

"It's OK for you to go out there with Ian," Jacob told him.

Toby ran over to him. The yellow treetops were still bright with the last of the sunlight.

"There's lots of leaves to rake!" Toby informed his dad as he kicked them around.

"I know," Jacob said grouchily from inside. He was keeping the back door open. It was warm in there from cooking so it was just as well.

Even after what happened at the funeral, Ian still didn't know where he stood with Lorna. Was that her? Did she really say goodbye? Seeing him looking toward the bench, Toby pulled on his sleeve.

"She went away. The lady. She had to go," Toby told him.

"Did you see her leave?" Ian asked.

"Her grandma came to get her," Toby said as if a ghost got picked up like a kid at the end of a school day.

"And she took her away somewhere?"

"Yes. Her grandma said, 'Let these nice people be. It's time to rest.' You think she means like a nap?" Toby asked.

"Kind of. It's good that she'll be with her grandma now."

"Yeah," Toby agreed. "She won't be lonely. And me and Dad have you now."

Ian smiled at his words, but he was surprised that hearing she was gone made him so sad. He knew that the Lorna who lingered here was just a remnant, not the real person who had once been his mother. The real Lorna was the one Ian wished he could meet.

He turned his eyes away from the empty space in the back garden and looked up at the evening sky. There was a bird singing somewhere high in the treetops, among the dry leaves. As he blinked back tears, Ian didn't know what he was supposed to feel about anything. That's when Toby took his hand. Ian looked down at his bright eyes and everything became simple and clear.

"I think I'd like to be a dad some day," Ian told him. He saw Jacob standing in the doorway, listening.

"First you have to get a kid," Toby informed him.

"Is that how it works?"

He nodded. Ian wished he could tell him that he wanted to be his dad. The more time he spent with Jacob and Toby, the more he wanted to barge in and demand a place in their little family.

Jacob knew what Ian was saying. He was smiling so maybe he could get behind the idea that even someone as young as him could be a halfway decent dad.

After dinner, they went for a walk and then Ian spent a quiet evening with Jacob and Toby. When it was Toby's bedtime, Jacob invited Ian to stay the night. Toby was very happy to hear Ian say yes.

There was a guest room and Ian poked his head in there a few hours later when he and Jacob were ready to call it a night.

"What are you doing in there?" Jacob asked him.

"I hate to mess it up for just one night," Ian said seeing the bed neatly made up. "I could just take the couch."

"What are you talking about? You're sleeping with me," Jacob told him. He sounded kind of bossy.

"What if I don't want to," Ian teased him.

"Really?"

"No, not really," Ian admitted. He needed the comfort of

being with Jacob more than he could say.

"I already told Toby you're my boyfriend, and I also told him that boyfriends sleep together," Jacob said as they went to his room.

Ian thought he might not want him to sleep over because of Toby, but that man was always surprising him.

Jacob was in the bathroom while Ian stripped out of his clothes. He decided to get in bed and wait for Jacob there. Climbing into his bed, knowing he was going to be spending the night, gave him such a good feeling.

When Jacob joined him and saw he was naked, he told him, "We don't have to do anything."

"Yes, we do. I need you," Ian told him. Though he appreciated how considerate Jacob was, Ian's whole being was aching for him.

"Remember to be quiet," Jacob told him.

"You too."

Ian reached out and freed Jacob of his pajama bottoms. Now his magnificent body was Ian's to touch and kiss all over. His lips, his tongue, his hands were sliding over every inch of him while his body was pressed up against Jacob, grinding into him. Jacob's touch electrified his skin, made him tremble with an almost painful need.

Getting condoms and lube with shaking hands, Ian told him, "Fuck me like only you can."

Jacob said nothing. He just kissed him so hard Ian felt like he was sinking into oblivion. Then his fingers got busy.

On his back, his legs pushed up, Ian writhed helplessly as Jacob's slick fingers merely circled his hole. The teasing dance ended with the slow press of Jacob's fingers until Ian's body allowed them in.

This time Jacob fingered him more gently than ever before. So why was it more excruciating? Because Ian wanted his cock and Jacob wasn't letting him have it. This was going to be an all night torture.

It was only minutes, but it seemed like forever. Then Jacob was warning him to be quiet and getting ready to enter him. Ian clenched his jaw and his breath hitched at the first thrust. He took inch after inch in silence, only breathing hard and looking up into Jacob's eyes.

That night, Jacob made love to him with long slow thrusts that went on forever. Ian could only whisper his name. He couldn't moan. He couldn't cry out. Knowing that holding back was agony, Jacob leaned down and kissed him.

Ian felt like he had never existed before this moment. Jacob was kissing him while his cock was driving jolts of pleasure deep inside him. Ian was lost to it. Every one of his senses, his body and soul, all of him belonged to Jacob.

He never knew anyone could get so deep inside him, or that he could give himself to anyone with such complete love and trust, nothing held back. Even when Jacob stopped kissing him, their connection was unbroken.

"You'll always be mine," Jacob told him as if he heard Ian silently promising himself to him.

"Yes," Ian said though it hadn't been a question.

Jacob started pumping harder. One powerful thrust followed another, each one drawing a silent moan and a shudder out of him. The whole time Ian's hips bucked up for more, because with Jacob, there was no such thing as enough. There was only "I love you" and Jacob's name whispered a thousand times as Ian drowned in the bottomless blue of his eyes.

*

No one had ever looked at him like that. As he was lost in Ian's turbulent gaze, Jacob existed only for him. He possessed and worshiped only him. They sweated and strained together and created this pure, perfect moment.

But their bodies wouldn't be denied. Edging closer to his climax, Jacob wanted to make the moment last. His cock was gripped in a vise of Ian's body. He had no choice but to come. Feeling his body start to tighten under him, he pumped harder. Ian's whole body was taut, so close to coming, and Jacob was right there with him.

Their bodies slammed together. Every hushed sound and movement combined into one wave of pure pleasure that raised them high above all the pain. Ian was surging under him, his head thrown back, his eyes wide, his scream silent.

Jacob whispered Ian's name. The sound of it was harsh, forced out of his throat as he was coming and trying not to scream out his name. Sweaty skin to skin, wallowing in the moment, and in each other, they were intimately connected, sharing the same pleasure.

Feeling like he was falling, Jacob covered Ian's body with his. Ian took his weight with a contented sigh, but then Jacob rolled off him. Ian didn't let him get far. He ran his hand over Jacob's arm. Entwining their fingers, he clasped their hands together. He rested his head on Jacob's chest.

"This is how I want to sleep," Ian said. Then Jacob put his arm around his back. "That's even better."

Jacob couldn't take his eyes off him as he slept. He was beautiful and he was his. Since he met him, Jacob was completely in his power and under his spell, and he was happy to remain that way for the rest of his life.

That first night Ian slept in his bed was like a dream. Though Ian was so sad, it might have been the best night of Jacob's life.

Early the next morning, Jacob untangled himself from Ian

who moaned unhappily but stayed asleep. He went to Toby's room to check on him. As he poked his head in, Jacob found Toby sideways on his bed, curled up in a way that never failed to make him smile. He looked like he had gotten into a fight with his blanket. Mouth open, sheets spilling off the bed, pillow under one arm, he was his sweet little guy.

Jacob decided to take advantage of his sleeplessness and make pancakes for breakfast. Not expecting Ian to wake up soon, he took his time and replayed last night over and over in his head. One moment he was doubting it could have been as good as he remembered. The next moment, he was shuddering at the memory of it.

Once Toby was awake and dying to dig into the pancakes, Jacob went to wake Ian. He hated to do it, but he sat on the edge of the bed and kissed his face until Ian's eyes opened.

His voice husky with sleep, Ian said, "Good morning." He wrapped himself around Jacob and tried to pull him down into bed with him.

"I'm not here for that. I'm calling you to breakfast," Jacob told him, resisting the pull and the attraction of that warm body he loved.

"Fuck breakfast," Ian said making another go at it. He tried to wrestle Jacob to the bed but failed.

When Ian showed up in the kitchen dressed but bleary-eyed, Jacob reminded him, "You did say one of your duties as a boyfriend was to eat pancakes with us."

"We can have pancakes every day," Toby said. He was already sitting at the table, a bottle of pancake syrup next to him, uncapped and ready to go.

"Wouldn't you get tired of pancakes?" Ian asked him.

Toby shook his head and gave him an incredulous look. "That can't ever happen," he assured Ian.

"Then sign us up for pancakes every day," Ian teased Jacob, who grumbled.

"Stop encouraging him," Jacob said.

"Who should stop encouraging who?" Ian asked.

"Both of you." As Jacob finished up the last of the pancakes and turned off the stove, he smiled to himself. His life seemed so much sweeter now. At one time, he thought he could make peace with short-term relationships and fleeting attachments as long as he had Toby. But he didn't know what he was missing. If he had known there was a guy out there who could make him feel like this, he would have torn apart the whole world looking for him.

Just as he was thinking how wonderful being with Ian was, he came over to him. Ian put his arm around him, kissed him and made it even better.

*

Waking up in Jacob's bed with Jacob kissing him was like a dream. And that was only the first time. From now on, they would kiss each other awake, wake in each other's arms, wake each other with blowjobs. If only Ian didn't have to go back to college next term.

Until then, Ian was going to be with Jacob and Toby as much as he could. That's why he went along as Jacob took Toby to school. Going on foot, they dropped off Toby at kindergarten. They walked back so Jacob could get the car and drive to work. Not wanting to part yet, they stood in front of Jacob's house, holding hands.

"Did you want to stay here with us until you go back to school?" Jacob asked.

"I'll stay at the house till the start of next term." Despite that, Ian knew he would be spending most of his time with Jacob and Toby. He did want to get the house in order, and he also didn't want to rush things. On second thought, maybe he did. He didn't have time to waste. He would be going back to college.

"Eventually we will need to figure out which house you guys want to live in – this one or my family's house outside of town," he told Jacob.

"What?" Jacob said, surprised. He held Ian's gaze in disbelief.

Ian looked back at him steadily then he said, "No rush. I'll be coming down from college a lot to see you guys. My house can be our love nest. Then we can be as loud as we want."

That didn't put Jacob at ease at all. "You sure are making a lot of plans," he griped.

"Just letting you know how it's gonna be from now on."

"I hate to think of you going away to school. It's too much time apart. Even one minute apart is too long," Jacob said, getting serious.

Ian grabbed the front of his jacket and pulled him close. "The wait will be worth it. I promise."

"OK. You mentioned eating pancakes. As my boyfriend, what else do you see yourself doing?" Jacob asked like it was a job interview. He gave Ian a challenging look. Who did he think he was dealing with?

"I'll be staying up with you late at night when you can't sleep. When you are cold because the blanket fell off the bed, I'll keep you warm. I'll tell you how good you smell then I'll lick you and tell you how good you taste. When..."

"You know I have to go to work. Does this list have an end?"

"No. It goes on forever. There are big things and small things on it, and I'll keep adding more till I die."

"You know how to seduce a guy," Jacob said, giving him a hint that he would be thinking about him all day long.

"It's me and you forever." Ian threw himself into his arms and kissed him.

As Jacob held him even tighter against him, he said, "I never want to let you go." Then he leaned in. His lips brushed across Ian's face and then his ear. "Will you marry me?" Jacob whispered the words like a secret.

Ian gasped and drew back. "You bastard. Yes!" Ian said and laughed through tears as Jacob kissed him.

"The wedding won't be happening for a while. You're still too young, and we haven't known each other that long. We might just implode. Consider yourself on probation," Jacob told him, getting all bossy and rational.

"Don't try to boss me around. You're on probation. Go to work," Ian told him with one last, quick kiss.

He watched Jacob drive away and waved at him. Then he thought better of it, and gave him the finger. He was going to be fun to be married to. Ian bet himself that he could get a wedding out of him before Christmas.

As Ian walked home, the morning air was cold but the sky was bright. Ian thought about his dad and about Lorna. He went home all mixed up, happy and sad, in love, and engaged.

THE END

GOLDEN DAYS

Luke has been working in a string of nightclubs for most of his adult life. It was an exciting life, but Luke had enough of it. A recent loss sends Luke into suburbia in search of a more peaceful life. The loss of his brother is still fresh, but spending time with Kyle and Viv brings him so much joy.

In the past, Kyle hasn't been lucky in love. He always goes for the wrong kind of guy. But with Viv in his life, he can't afford those kinds of mistakes.

How can a nerdy, young dad hope to attract his hunky new neighbor? And if he can get his attention, does he have any hope of making it last?

Kyle only recently became an adoptive father to a vulnerable little girl. He's a devoted dad, and Viv is a spirited and loving five-year-old. With the help of his little dog, Kyle worked hard to gain Viv's love and trust in record time. Now they are a family. That doesn't mean he has no room for a man in his life.

When Luke moves into the neighborhood, Kyle ends up with two wounded souls on his hands. Good thing he has room in his heart for both of them. If Kyle can get past his fears, he might just get everything he has always dreamed of.

WHERE HE BELONGS

Jack thought he had everything only to end up without a wife, a best friend or a child. Now he is closed off and afraid to love. After despair nearly cost him his life, he can't afford another heartbreak. Burying himself in work, Jack has made business his whole life. Now a business opportunity has led him to Gus, the one man who can break down his defenses.

Gus doesn't know what he is getting himself into when he flirts with his new boss. The uptight younger man is irresistible to him. Is Gus being reckless when he falls for Jack despite all the warning signs? After all, Gus is a happy, single father to a little boy, and Josh is a happy kid.

As he is drawn into their lives, Jack finds that Gus and his little boy are everything he needs and what he is most afraid of. Jack can't risk his heart again, but he might be won over by these two goofballs despite himself.

HIS TRUE HOME

Alec has retreated to his childhood home after a life of too much fun. When a little boy is abandoned on the road leading to Alec's home town of Seaview Pines, Alec is the one who ends up taking care of him. Now Cory is on his way to join them. He was abandoned by his mother as well and wants to give Teddy, his little brother, the family he never had. As they spend time together, it's up to Cory to draw out the serious, silent little boy. He also has to convince Alec that his home town isn't just a temporary refuge. It's where all three of them belong.

LONG LOST

Blake Adler is back in town on a mission. Years ago Blake's father cut him out of his life so completely that he never spoke of him. Now that his father has passed away, Blake finally gets to meet his younger brother and sister. But Blake didn't come back to Meadowview for a reunion with his lost family. He's desperate to find the man he can't live without and win back the love he threw away.

Blake and Reese were once best friends. They could have been more, but Blake screwed up the most important relationship of his life. Now he wants to fix things with Reese, if he can only find him.

Blake isn't the only one looking for Reese. No matter how far Reese runs, trouble follows him. Wild and vulnerable, he always had it rough. The one good thing in his life was Blake.

Now Reese is taking a big risk coming back to town. It might be worth it if he can reclaim the man he can't stop thinking about, the one who rejected him, the one he loves more than anyone.

MANNY TO THE RESCUE

Why would Owen be terrified of Connie and Maggie, his two adorable little nieces? Because he is about to be left alone with them. Owen thinks he is going to have to take care of his nieces by himself until Dan shows up. If Owen approves, Dan is ready to be the girls' manny. Right from the start, Dan is a big help and an even bigger temptation. And Owen isn't the only one being tempted. When he was younger, Dan had a crush on Owen. Now that he is living with him, Owen has never looked hotter. The crush is back in full force. Too bad Dan isn't the kind of guy Owen is into. But even a hint that he is interested might spur Dan to make a move. Unfortunately, Dan is bringing trouble with him, and he doesn't even know it. When Owen becomes a target, will Dan be there in time to save him?

HIS WINTER HEART

Wes is living a lonely, stark existence when he meets Colin, a lively young guy in desperate circumstances. Wes is so taken with him that he has to have him. His decision to invite Colin to spend the night is going to turn his quiet life upside down.

Colin almost finds himself sleeping on the street. When the tall, blond man makes him an offer, he can't say no either to the money or to the man. Colin is impulsive and full of contradictions. He refuses to sell himself for money and ends up homeless because of it. But when Wes offers to pay him for sex, Colin jumps at the chance to go home with him. Something about Wes strikes a chord with Colin. He knows there is a warm heart under the serious, impassive exterior and an awesome body under all the layers of winter clothes.

Things don't go as planned when Wes decides that Colin is too young and inexperienced and refuses to sleep with him. That doesn't mean that he can stay away from someone who shakes up his world.

The more time Colin spends with Wes, the more he wants him. Colin isn't shy about getting what he wants. His relentless pursuit might pay off if Wes doesn't let family complications and his fears about the future keep them apart. Will Wes let go of his inhibitions and allow himself to love the younger man?

POISON HEART

Is there anything Vince and Cal won't do for each other? The two of them grew up together and fell deeply in love. They were poor but happy until Cal made a big mistake and ended up in jail. He did it for Vince. To get him out, Vince is willing to do anything. Roland Granger has the power and influence to make Cal a free man. All he wants in return is Vince. Even if Cal never forgives him, Vince is willing to sacrifice himself. Now he has to make sure that Cal accepts this unwanted help. And while Vince is trying to set things right in his own life, can he reunite Roland with a self-destructive young man who loves him?

AND MANNY MAKES THREE

Mark is a struggling college student who has been working as a nanny for a nice family, but they don't need him any more. Zack has been raising his son, Al, by himself and needs help. Al is a funny kid, and Zack is a funny dad, but more serious issues lurk under the surface. Will Mark be able to deal with these two? And how will Zack and Mark deal with their mutual attraction?

UNEXPECTED DAD

Tyler finds a big surprise waiting on his doorstep. Ready or not, Tyler is a dad. Tyler didn't know he had a daughter until she suddenly dropped into his life. Whether he is ready for her or not, little Julie needs a father. Or maybe two. Tyler and Jake have been best friends, inseparable since college. Now they have to adjust to Tyler's new role as a dad. As Jake helps him cope with being a new father to a little girl, Tyler might be looking at two big changes in his life.

MORE THAN A MANNY

A very young, rich widower needs a nanny, but a hot manny would be even better. That's where Nate comes in. Brent is a loving but irresponsible father to two young children from a marriage of convenience. He needs Nate in his life, but how will Nate, a first time nanny, fit into his unconventional household? The kids are a handful, especially little Georgie. Her big brother, Ricky, has a few issues of his own. But Nate is more than ready to take on the challenge and let all three of them steal his heart.

DUNCAN THE THIRD

Patrick and his little sister, Wendy, have just moved into Duncan's building and that means trouble. Patrick is exactly the kind of guy Duncan can't resist. Together he and his little sister might be the family Duncan has been yearning for but only if he takes a chance and lets them into his heart. Unfortunately, Duncan hasn't been lucky when it comes to relationships. After getting his heart broken too many times, he has sworn off younger men. While Duncan struggles against his attraction to him, Patrick is determined to win him over. As Patrick tries to change his mind, can he also heal Duncan's broken heart?

MAKE IT BETTER

A favor leads to a life changing experience. Ray is willing to do anything for the man he considers his savior. His mission of mercy is Marcus, a young man who can't overcome his guilt over a tragedy in his past. Is Ray making a terrible mistake giving his heart to him, or will his love for Marcus be strong enough to save him?

THE RIGHT GUY

They came together in paradise, but what will happen when they go back to the real world and their everyday lives?

Nathan and Paul never liked each other. Paul was a snob, and Nathan felt like he was always looking down on him. Nathan wasn't interested in him anyway. He had his sights set on Turner. Now that Turner is getting married to another man, Nathan's heart is breaking. That's when he finds that Paul is right there by his side. This gorgeous man is ready to distract him and help him get over his unrequited crush.

After being with Paul, Nathan is finally ready to move on and let go of his hopeless feelings. But after a hot encounter on the beach, Nathan might be giving up his old crush for a new one. Knowing that his longing for Paul is just as hopeless, Nathan is at his wit's end.

But things aren't the way they seem. Paul has been watching Nathan pine after his friend for too long. All that time he has wanted Nathan all to himself. It's hard for Paul to believe that Nathan could ever return his feelings. After all, Nathan doesn't even like him.

He doesn't know that Nathan feels differently about him these days. When spending time with Paul stirs unexpected feelings that are more than lust, Nathan wonders if he misjudged this man. Could Paul be the right man for him? After chasing the wrong guy for so long, Nathan has to prove to Paul that his feelings are real. That won't be easy. Paul isn't the most reasonable guy, and he won't settle for anything less from Nathan than his whole heart.

POSSESSION

While looking for solitude, James finds love.

As soon as he arrives at the secluded, tropical villa, James knows he has found the ideal spot. Tranquil and remote, this place is just what he needs to get over a painful breakup. In perfect solitude, James's heart can begin to heal. But what if his solitude isn't so perfect, and Rob is. He is the young man who intrudes on James's privacy and steals his heart.

Rob is too much of a temptation for the cautious and uptight James. Even as he gives in to his desire, James reminds himself that this is just a vacation fling. Then why is the thought of leaving Rob tearing him apart? He can't get enough of the younger man. Once James has his body, he can't live without having his heart.

James thinks his yearning is hopeless. Then a revelation about Rob's circumstances changes everything. Will James have the courage to act on his feelings? He has to. This is his chance to have Rob, to give him the life he deserves and to truly love him.

15949857R00093

Printed in Great Britain
by Amazon